Lanyards & Lariats

Working for Love, Book 1

Amber W. Lynne

Carnelian & Quills Publishing

Edited by: Krissy Espindola (KrissyEspindola@gmail.com)
Cover Art by: Rebecca Ruger (BeckandDot@gmail.com)
Paper: ISBN 978-1-960479-17-4
eBook: ISBN 978-1-960479-16-7
Text Copyright © 2025 by Carnelian & Quills Publishing
All rights reserved.

This book is dedicated in loving memory to Jen...who worked really damn hard to make love work.

"The course of true love never did run smooth."
A Midsummer Night's Dream
William Shakespeare

Chapter One

Bailey

Her father had won.

Bailey threw the morning paper down on the table, cussed, and then snatched it back up.

There she was—staring back from the front page. The photo was old: platinum-blonde curls framing her heart-shaped face, polished and pristine. It made her look way younger than her thirty-five years, but it also pissed her off. That girl wasn't her anymore.

Hugh "Rusty" Reynolds III, patriarch of the family, had decided that Sherry Ann Reynolds' obituary would feature their perfect daughter. Did it even cross his mind to ask if she wanted her name—let alone her face—plastered across the front page?

Her mom had been planning for her death for over a year. From the orchids at the memorial to the canapes served at the wake, Sherry knew what she'd wanted. Although it wasn't cancer, she vowed to accept whatever came her way in life. Bailey had promised her mom a picture book perfect ending, but this felt like her father was violating her privacy. Hugh was more than aware that she didn't like the press.

Instead, the old coot let Sherry write whatever she wanted and then tied it up with a big fat bow for the papers. Rusty would do anything to make their family name look better. The obituary mentioned nothing about the funeral arrangements, but a brief note suggested that, instead of flowers, mourners could send gifts to a local homeless shelter.

Without information, she'd be calling Clinton, their family attorney. "No." She shook her head and threw the paper back down on the worn laminate table. Her truck keys lay in the basket at the table's center. Instead of reaching for the paper a third time, she grabbed them, took five steps to the door, and then fifteen to her truck.

It growled to life, and she was spitting gravel before she'd even pulled on her seatbelt. Music pumped from the radio. A heady mix of guitar and fiddle. The bass gave her a steady beat to focus on as she drove the old blue Ford F-150 down the dirt lane. The truck passed acre after acre of lush green farmland. All that grass and land was another part of her mother's legacy. One she'd been so glad to share with her daughter. A herd of cattle grazed on her left, and she honked at them. They didn't stop chewing to even notice her.

When the song stopped, replaced by an annoying announcer selling mattresses, she turned the radio off. Oppressive silence was worse than the radio commercial. Tires crunched and bit into the edge of the road. She turned the engine off. "You bastard!" she said, hitting the steering wheel. Over and over, she slammed her hand into the dash until her palm ached.

When she stopped, her hand was red, and her throat was raw. "I wasn't ready." With a hand on each side, she dropped her forehead and gripped the steering wheel until her knuckles were white. The heat building up in the cab forced her to lift her head and turn the key. "Fine." She gritted her teeth, turned the truck back around, and drove home.

"Ms. Reynolds, I was hoping to speak with you sooner, but you never returned my calls."

"I stopped answering calls from lawyers after my ex tried to take me for everything I owned."

"And, as I remember it, you should be happily answering my calls and thanking me for what we pulled off."

"Whatever. A hack out of law school could have won that case. He cheated on me with half the women he met."

"Right, but he also had an ironclad prenuptial. Which, I'll remind you, I advised you not to sign."

"Thanks for the walk down memory lane, Clint, but that's not why I called."

He cleared his voice, and it rumbled across the line. "Clinton, or Mr. Conners, if you don't mind."

"Sure. You know why I called, Mr. Conners."

"It's truly unfortunate. You have my deepest sympathies." There were the muffled sounds of a woman's voice, and the rasping sound of paper shuffling. "Your mother has been...was...a client here for many years."

The kitchen wasn't large enough for her to pace. With a quick push, she shoved open the screen door and stepped onto the wrap-around porch. "Just lay it out."

"I have explicit instructions to wait."

"On what?" Her feet crunched in the rocky driveway and her voice startled the chickens nearby. Their squawks forced her around the backside of the house.

"You'll need to attend the memorial service and there will be a reading of your mother's Last Will and Testament on Friday."

The tire swing hanging off the tree in the old house's backyard rocked in the soft breeze. "This Friday? Like this week? But, I—"

"You knew this was coming, Ms. Reynolds. It would have helped if you'd answered my phone calls." He took a deep breath that whistled in her ear. "The memorial is Thursday afternoon, and the reading of the Will is the next morning."

"My contact info is the same. Send me the details and I'll be there." A rumbling in the distance caught her attention as she finished walking around the house. "I have to go."

He was sputtering on the line when she hung up, but she didn't have time to worry about being rude. As the large yellow bus rumbled up to the end of the driveway, she watched the doors open wide and her daughter bounced out. The afternoon light shimmered off the sun-kissed ponytail and sweet pink cheeks of the little girl that looked so much like her at that age.

"Hey Rosie, how was school?"

"The best!" she said, taking Bailey's outstretched hand.

She gripped her daughter's small hand and then took a deep

breath. "Let's go get you a snack. We need to talk."

Chapter Two

Bailey

"How was the flight?"

"What?" Bailey rolled her shoulders and shifted her purse from her right side to her left. She could barely hear her friend over the busy sounds of traffic and the people shuffling past her on the sidewalk. "Is Rosie okay?"

"Of course! We'll be fine. Do what you have to do there."

"I left cash for food." The New York buildings towered around Bailey as she swerved around the other pedestrians walking down Barclay Street. Her father wanted the service at St. Patrick's, but even Hugh hadn't been able to pull that off.

"I already spent it on delivery pizza and a movie for tonight. We're fine, Bailey, I promise."

"Your voice isn't right." An elbow bumped her, and she side-stepped a foot that was in her path. The church's towers were barely visible two blocks up. "Candy, what's wrong?"

"It's nothing to do with you or Rosie."

When a honking taxi drowned out her daughter's laughter

in her ear, Bailey gripped the phone tighter.

"See, she's fine," said Candice into the phone. Her voice dropped almost too low for Bailey to hear. "I got a letter in the mail today from the bank."

"Again? I'm sorry." Another horn honked. Bailey raised her voice and said, "I can't talk now. I'm almost there. You should have said something yesterday."

"I know, but I didn't want to bother you."

Bailey ran a hand through her blonde hair and yanked the strap of her purse higher on her shoulder. The crowd was growing thick around her, and she could hardly hear Candice's voice over the sounds of the city.

"Grab some napkins and put in the movie." Candice spoke gently to Rosie, then told Bailey, "Don't worry about me. We'll figure it out when you get home."

Bailey held the phone tighter. "I promise. I love you. Thank you."

With one last goodbye to Rosie, she hung up the phone and climbed the steps of St. Thomas's church. The ancient gothic stone walls loomed over her as she pushed through its arching doors and entered the sanctuary. Candles illuminated every corner. Giant bouquets of roses, lilies, and tulips filled the air with the smell of spring. The flowers were beautiful. Her mother must have interviewed every musician in the city to find the harpist.

Churches were for mourning loss and penitent worship. The hard wood seats and cold stone walls reminded Bailey of all her father's sins. Perhaps the restlessness in her bones came from feeling a little guilty for herself. It would have been easy to blame her late afternoon flight for her late arrival at her mom's memorial, but she'd been procrastinating when she booked it.

Her subconscious must have known that it would be best for her to show up late, or she might have failed to make it at all. With cowboy boots still red from farm dirt, she sat down as the harpist played her first note. She wondered if she should have worn something other than her boots to a funeral, but her mom would have liked that, too.

Deep bass tones and tinkling high notes mixed to fill the space with calming, heavenly music. Sherry would've liked that, but she wouldn't have been fond of the pastor talking for over 20 minutes. By the time the preacher invited the guests up to the pulpit, people in their seats were twitching. It was no surprise that everyone chose compliments and lamentations. There weren't a lot of ill words to describe Sherry Ann Reynolds. Perhaps her mom planned that, too. No one mentioned that Sherry had grown agoraphobic in her old age or that she'd never been brave enough to tell her husband to shut up.

The guests spoke about her mother's countless volunteer hours and the dozens of benefit parties she'd thrown to help those in need. They didn't mention how Sherry grew up on a small cattle farm named The Ladder H in Serenity, Texas. Bailey knew that, if you'd asked Sherry when she was little where she wanted to raise her babies, she'd have told you right there in Serenity in the house next to her mama's. Bailey wanted to raise Rosie at that farm, too.

The dreams of little girls never last, and, within a few years of marrying Rusty Reynolds, he had moved Sherry to New York City and demanded everyone call him Hugh. That was decades ago. He saw the potential in their small family still. Business ran in his blood, and if he wasn't making money, he wasn't happy. Sherry's brothers were awful moonshiners. When things were hard at the Ladder H, they'd make a batch to earn a few bucks, but most of the time, they were too busy drinking their booze to sell it. Hugh insisted that the big city was what they needed to grow and expand, and he'd been right.

Hugh ensured Sherry Ann Harris was more than the daughter of a crappy cattle farmer and an infamous moonshine distiller. He'd turned the Harris family's illegal backyard still into a full-fledged legal operation. The nicest thing you could say about her father was that he was an extremely successful entrepreneur. Over the years, they moved from making moonshine that would clean the crud off your boots to producing whiskey that was in demand around the world. Ladder H Distilling became one of the largest importers and exporters of liquor in the United States.

Bailey's mom went from hosting Sunday brunches on their back patio in Serenity to catering exclusive dinners in their Manhattan penthouse in New York. Those were the people who filled the church pews. Bailey looked around at all the fancy hats and double-breasted suits.

There wasn't one other person from Serenity in that church. Sherry died living her lie. In Bailey's thirty years of living, her mom had only ever hinted once that her life hadn't gone the way she'd hoped. When Bailey showed up, covered in bruises with a baby in her arms, her mother gave her the keys to their Texas farm and said, "Go home, honey. One of us needs to make sure our roots stay strong and grow."

Now, sitting in that dimly lit church and listening to the pastor whisper quiet words about her mother, Bailey watched Hugh as he sat in the front of a room full of people mourning his wife and looking like he was out to Sunday dinner. The only thing he loved more than his company was himself, but her mom was a good Southern girl and would never admit that she wasn't grateful for everything he'd done. He made her family's business a success. Ultimately, though, it left Bailey sitting there in that stuffy church cathedral in New York, with too many flowers, too many people, and no one else there wearing Ariats.

As the pastor finished his speech, and the harpist plucked her last string, the mourners stood and filed out of the building. Her father and ex-husband walked by the pew where she sat. Over the head of a woman wearing a ridiculously large purple hat, she looked into her dad's cold eyes. Was that hatred? Intolerance? She didn't know what the hell it was, but she knew it made her feel 12 years old again.

With one finger, he gestured for her to follow, but, in an act of defiance, she waited. Two breaths. One more and then she rose from her seat. Packed into the exiting crowd, she watched him leave the building. When she made it to the old cathedral's entrance, the evening's sun rays shone on her face. Hugh was entering a long black limousine at the bottom of the church stairs. He'd be angry that he had to wait, but she couldn't get past the groups of mingling people and tearful mourners.

When she neared the car, the door opened, and a lone arm waved her in. Ducking her head into the dark interior of the vehicle, she slid into the cold leather seats and looked up at a pair of green eyes she hadn't seen in almost eight years. Once, she thought they held love for her. Now, she knew they were as cold and hard as the emeralds they resembled.

"You could show some respect for the dead and actually show up on time."

"Dad, I don't think I'm the one who should apologize for disrespecting mom."

"You know your mother valued punctuality."

"Yeah, she also valued fidelity."

"Don't you take that tone with me. I wasn't the one who showed up late to the funeral."

Taking a deep breath, she consciously unclasped her hands. "Well, thank you for the lesson in manners. I will remember that at the next funeral I attend." She refrained from mentioning the fact that he never even told her the funeral was happening. Thanks to Clinton, she'd arrived mostly on time.

"Bailey, you know your father is trying to help you." Her ex-husband's voice sounded like summer rain on a porch roof. It was soothing and rumbled with a soft, but unpredictable, beat. Business owners from all over the world fell for the promises he made in that whiskey-smooth voice.

"Right." It made her feel less alone when she thought about all the other people who fell for his lies.

The dim light of the car softened Ethan's face. He almost didn't look like an asshole. His short-cropped hair and tailored suit made him look every inch like the dashing professional that he was.

The fabric of her knee length sundress pulled at her chest when she sat tall and pulled back her shoulders. "I see the two of you are still thick as thieves."

"Ethan makes an excellent business partner. I've always been able to rely on him."

It was impossible to miss the emphasis he placed on the word him. She knew better than to engage with her dad. Her mom had always stepped between them. It took Bailey a long time to find her voice. She went from an abusive father to an abusive husband, and it wasn't until she walked away with Rosie that she swore she would never let another man treat her like that again.

The engine started, and the car began to roll forward. Through the back window, she could see the procession of vehicles lining up behind their limousine. For her mother's sake, she needed to remain civil. Speaking never worked, anyhow. She knew that nothing she said would ever matter to her dad or her ex-husband. Tucked in the corner, she saw the small minibar. Her eyes looked at the glasses that rattled gently as the car moved down the road, and her hands slid down the soft cotton lace of her dress.

"How was your flight? How's Rosie doing?"

Casual conversation with her ex was the last thing she wanted to be doing on the way to her mother's gravesite. "She's sad, but we've all known this was coming. The flight was packed. I'm lucky there weren't any delays," she said, then leaned back into the seat to watch the string of cars following behind them.

"Well, you should have brought her with you. Her grandmother would have liked that. It wouldn't have hurt for the press to see us as a united family."

The word family made her stomach flip. Bailey refused to take the bait. If she was going to play these games with her father, she would need to keep her wits about her. The drink she so desperately wanted would need to wait.

Chapter Three

Mac

When Mac pushed through O'Toole's door with Mitch hanging off his right arm and Greg swaying on his left, he'd only meant to kill an hour and keep two idiots out of handcuffs.

Lately, even his quiet apartment above the bar felt too loud with thoughts he couldn't turn off—snatches of headlines, the hammer of gunfire, and a montage of hungry faces. Round after round wouldn't fix any of it, but dragging his friends home afterward would at least feel useful.

Mitch was bumping his right side, and he was steadying Greg with his left. They'd had too much to drink three bars back, but there was no way they were letting him tap out now. Heading to O'Toole's had seemed like an excellent compromise. Since it was a few steps to his apartment, he hoped he could pour them into bed after one last round.

The sexy blonde at the bar had been unexpected. Boots hooked on the stool rungs, shoulders squared like she dared the room to try her, a blonde sat at the far end of the bar. She slid a card across the sticky counter. "Screwdriver. Make it a double."

The bartender set a drink down with a nod, then cocked his chin at Mac as he walked past. "Hey, Hero. Make sure those friends of yours don't cause any trouble tonight." Pete always had a way of turning a greeting into a warning.

"From the gentleman," Pete added to the blonde, pushing her card back.

"I don't—" she said, and then looked down the length of the bar. An elderly gentleman sat in the last seat, concealed in the shadows. He held up two fingers of something honey colored in the bottom of a lowball glass. "Fine do it," she said, and held up her glass, miming the toast, then she tossed back a long gulp of the drink.

Before the half-empty glass could hit the bar, the guy appeared next to her. "Hi, I'm Jeremy. First time here?"

"First and last," she said, then softened it with a dry smile. "Thanks for the drink."

"Come on, Mac!" Mitch bellowed behind him, pulling his attention away from the woman. "Not a pub crawl if you don't crawl."

"I am drinking. I just haven't gotten to the crawl part," Mac said, easing them toward the counter. When they bellied up to the bar, Jeremy realized he was out of his league and faded back into the darkness at the end of the bar, but his occasional glances showed he was still interested. Mac couldn't blame him for not wanting to engage with the aged-out, drunken frat boys.

He glanced at Pete and lowered his voice. "How many has she had?"

"That was her first." A warm flush covered her cheeks, and

she was sitting slightly tilted in her seat. "Better pour them lighter from now on."

Pete nodded and went back to moderating the debate Greg and Mitch were having. "No. You're wrong, the New York Jets could take on the Patriots any day."

Mac turned back to her as a barstool clattered behind him. She began slipping on her stool, but she steadied herself before falling.

He wanted to stay with her, but his buddies wouldn't make it much longer without being arrested, or at least causing a scene that good ole' Pete would never let them forget.

He was looking for an opening to introduce himself when she said, "Seems like the guys are having fun."

"Yeah," he said, offering half a smile. "Sorry about them. They're only looking for a good time."

"Of course." She tipped her glass toward the commotion. "I wasn't looking for a good time, so I'm thrilled they're having it for me."

He couldn't help it—he laughed. Sarcasm looked good on her. "You here alone?"

"I'm not alone." She cut him a look that landed somewhere between challenge and invitation. "I have you."

He was close enough to catch the citrus from her drink and something honeyed that was all her. Up close, she was striking—clean lines, heart-shaped mouth, a set to her jaw that said she wasn't taking crap from anyone. "Malcolm," he said, offering his hand. "If you're mad at me. My friends call me—"

"Mac," she finished, sliding her palm against his. "Bailey."

"Bailey?" Mac asked.

"It's a family tradition to name the kids after liquor."

"Better than a vegetable." His smile was so genuine, she couldn't help laughing. He felt that one in his chest. "Rough day?" he asked.

"Funeral," she said, simple as a slap. "My mother's. With my narcissistic father and control-abusing ex-husband." She tossed back another swallow and set the glass a little harder than she'd meant to. "Probably TMI, but that tells you how much I needed that drink."

Mac ignored the pinch behind his ribs. "Looks like you're almost done. Can I get you another as an apology for my crew?"

"I'm on a roll." She eyed him over the rim. "But don't think I'm going home with you."

"Noted." He gestured to Pete with a telling wink. *Light.* "One more?" When the glass slid across, Bailey didn't touch it.

"Why aren't you celebrating with them?" she asked, chin tipping toward Mitch and Greg as they tried to sell a pool game to a woman who'd already said no twice.

"Differing views on what we should celebrate," he said. "I was in Uganda the last six months. They're glad I'm home, but I wonder if I shouldn't have stayed over there."

She watched him, sharper now. "Backstory?"

"I'm a journalist," he said. "I write stories so people don't slip through the cracks."

"Sure you do. Along with every other journalist in that space."

He dragged a finger through the condensation on his beer. Let her see it or don't, he thought. No speeches. "Without a voice, those people are all but forgotten."

Her gaze caught his, and for a beat the room narrowed to the length of the bar and the set of her mouth. She looked like someone who'd learned how to carry more than her share. "You didn't let me slip," she said. "You've already rescued me, and I've only been here half an hour."

"Rescue?" He shook his head. "You're not the type. I'm just lucky you're still talking to me."

She tilted, the stool wobbling; his hand came up, ready, then hovered when she caught herself. "How are you feeling?"

"Like I want to dance," she said, clear and sudden, a spark under the ash. "I need a small sliver of joy so strong it hurts."

"There's more there."

"There is," she said. "For three hundred and sixty-five days I waited for a phone call telling me my mother was gone. I said goodbye every day, just in case." She swallowed, her throat working. "Today I watched them lower her into the ground. I got to love her all year. Now I need to dance."

He didn't argue.

The scarred hardwood beneath their boots wasn't usually used for dancing, but Mac made them space between the beer-stained tables. Bailey fit perfectly in his arms—tighter than she probably realized—her head nestled just under his chin. Her blonde curls brushing against his jaw every time she swayed.

The easy beat of the jukebox track wrapped around them like a long exhale, steady as water lapping against a dock. The soles of her well-worn Ariats moved in lazy circles across the floor, brushing the tips of his boots. Every subtle sway pressed her body into his, warm and impossible to ignore. He noticed the way she melted a little more with each measure of the song.

Her walls weren't down, not totally, but maybe they'd tilted.

"The last time I danced like this was at my wedding," she said, voice low.

He leaned back an inch to see her face. "The ex from today?"

"Yeah." She said it like she'd prepared for the flinch.

"If leaving felt right," he said, holding her eyes, "you probably didn't come to it lightly."

Her boot skimmed his. "Never mind," she said, and then tucked it away.

"Bailey—" he held back. *What made this girl as intoxicating as her name?*

When the jukebox clicked and a new song kicked on—wailing harmonica and sharp country twang—Mac felt the shift in her before she moved. Something snapped loose. The sad-eyed woman wrapped in his arms turned wild and electric.

Like a flipped switch, Bailey disengaged, bent slightly, and started letting go. She kicked off one boot, then the other. One landed against the nearby table leg with a thud. Barefoot now, she curled her toes against the slick wood floor and began to move with unselfconscious, tipsy abandon.

She bounced once, twisted the blue cotton dress over her hips, and let her arms float out wide like she was soaking in the song's beat.

Mac took half a step back, stunned. Her eyes closed, face tipped upward like she was worshiping old O'Toole's ceiling tiles. Her skin glowed under the colored lights spilling down from above.

She laughed—soft, free, not meant for anyone but herself—and spun in a slightly lopsided circle, blond curls flying.

Hell.

He wasn't sure when he started grinning, but his cheeks hurt enough to prove it. From across the room, he caught Mitch elbowing Greg and nodding in Mac's direction.

"Uh-oh," Greg said, slurring just enough to be obvious. "He's in trouble."

"Look! She's barefoot," Mitch laughed. "He's gonna marry her."

"Shut up," Mac muttered under his breath, eyes completely locked on the dervish in front of him.

Bailey turned back, eyes bright. She crooked a finger. *Come on.*

He went. Her hand was smaller than he expected, with a hint of callus that surprised him. He caught her on the hip as she spun. Her laughter caught in her throat and bounced right into his chest. He was already too far gone.

"Can I kiss you?" he asked, his voice barely above a whisper, laced with a raw yearning that made his heart pound. The muscles in his neck tightened as he waited, each drawn breath stretching into an eternity. He was captivated by the subtle movements of her lips, which were becoming more vital to him than the very air he breathed.

"Yes," she said, and it cracked something open. He bent to her, slow at first. The first press was soft, then truer when she lifted on her toes and met him there. Heat threaded tight between them. When she leaned closer, his hand flexed against the curve of her waist.

"I'll never look at another sundress without thinking of you," he said, and felt the tiny hitch in her breath before it faded.

"I wish this didn't have to end," she said.

"Maybe it doesn't."

"Maybe." She grazed his bottom lip with a playful bite that made his pulse stutter—and then Mitch yelled his name.

"Mac! Shots are gone. Greg lost the eight ball. Also maybe the nine. Help."

He closed his eyes for a beat. Of course. When he opened them, she was already bracing for him to go.

"I need to take them home," he said, hating the words and the way her mouth tipped at the corner like she'd expected it. Automatically, his hands pulled her closer again. "No."

"Mac," she said, the fight and softness braided together. "Thanks for tonight."

"They're just ribbing me," he lied, because they were, and because this felt like it mattered too much to leave on a joke. "I live upstairs. You could—"

"I'm not going up with you."

He shook his head. "I wasn't... They belong in a taxi. Please. Sit with Pete. Give me five minutes." He held her face in his palm so she could see he meant it. "We're going to finish what we started."

She studied him, then nodded once. "Five."

"That's all I need," he said, and turned toward the chaos, already calculating the fastest path to the door and the longest five minutes of his life.

Chapter Four

Bailey

Small gnomes were beating their itty-bitty pickaxes into the very center of her brain, and the last time she hated the sun so much was after her last optometry appointment when she'd spent two hours with her eyes dilated. What had she been thinking? New York dive bars, drinks, and wild dancing with strangers was not her thing. She'd lost her dang mind last night. It hadn't been letting off steam; it had been vomiting twenty years of resentment and hurt into a bar full of strangers.

The only thing she'd done right last night was leave the bar before Mac came back. Her gut knotted with the smallest twist of guilt when she thought about how he must have felt when he returned. Pete promised he would pass along her apologies, but he looked a little smug at the same time.

Chugging a glass of water seemed to help. The bathroom mirror showed her just how dumb she'd been last night. Hair that was normally smooth and neat was falling out of a knotted ponytail. She had mascara smeared around her eyes. Instead of looking like a cute panda, she looked more like an NFL football player gearing up for a game.

That was fitting, perhaps. The last place she wanted to be this morning, aside from standing in front of Mac apologizing, was Clinton's office. His glass-encased castle, with its marble tables and mahogany desks, was the main stage for most of her life's worst moments. Hate was a strong word, but she wanted something even more biting to describe the savage bitterness that washed through her when she thought of showing up there today.

Bailey looked out at the New York skyline and sighed. When she was young and full of hope and a childish need to please, that view excited her. Every party, benefit luncheon, gala, and soirée meant new friends and a chance to see some place bigger than the last. That was how she'd met Ethan Moore. She was going to be Mrs. Moore, and he was going to be her Prince Charming. Instead, he ended up playing the role of the villain, which was surprising since that part was usually reserved for her father.

The last time she'd walked the lush, carpeted hallways of Clinton's high-rise office, she'd been fighting her prenup for an inch of grace. In reality, she'd been signing her life away. She gave away the dripping diamonds, the neon-lit nights, and the flowing silk gowns...every single material trapping...all to protect Rosie. Her husband traded his family for the life he'd always wanted, and she'd happily given it all away. He ended up with all the respect and money, but she left their marriage with the one thing she'd never had as a child—a home.

Sherry had warned her, when her conceit and vanity hit unmanageable levels, that their roots were in Texas soil. Despite being brought up in the limelight with fur stoles, expensive jewels, and extravagant parties, Bailey's family originated from open fields, warm dusty afternoons, and living off the land. She hated that...when her mother reminded her of how simple they were.

A tap on her shoulder pulled her back to the present. "Ms. Reynolds, we're about ready for you."

Bailey turned to look at the tall, dark man standing behind her. He was in his mid-fifties. The morning sun brightened the silver gray of his temples and the wrinkles that spread from the corners of his eyes. He possessed an aged handsomeness that rivaled most Hollywood stars she'd seen. "Do you ever get tired of fixing my family's problems, Clint?"

"Clinton," he corrected, but Bailey could see the sparkle in his eyes. Maybe he was lightening up. "Mrs. Reynolds came to me before she married your father...before he was Hugh and he still let people call him Rusty. I was fresh out of law school. My office was barely 900 square feet and part of a strip mall in New Jersey." He glanced out at the morning sun glinting off skyscrapers and flooding the office with sunshine. "When The Ladder H offices moved to New York, I followed your family here. The windowless basement office off Wall Street was a reputable address, but it was a long way from where we are now."

"Why Clinton?"

"It has been an honor watching you grow up."

"I barely..."

A muscle twitched in Clinton's jaw. His eyes were cold when he looked at her. "No, Ms. Reynolds." He shook his head one time. "Sherry made this company, but what you did was even harder. I'm sorry–"

A cute brunette opened a dark mahogany door a few feet away. "Mr. Conner, we're ready when you are."

"Ms. Reynolds, are you ready?"

"Maybe..."

He placed his hand on her shoulder. "When we're done here...please know, the company pays my retainer, not your father."

Bailey glanced at Clinton and said, "What does that mean?"

"It's time," he said, and walked away.

As he walked through the door the secretary had popped out of, she could see Ethan, Hugh, and their entourage seated around the long boardroom table. "Lord, save me..." she mumbled and took a deep breath before following Clinton into the lion's den.

Chapter Five

Bailey

"Unacceptable!" Hugh shouted and slammed his palm on the table.

Just an octave below him was Ethan's astounded reply. "You're kidding. This is a joke, right?" He pointed an angry finger at Bailey's face and growled at Clinton. "What's she supposed to do with the company?"

Bailey watched in shock. It took three breaths before she could choke out even simple words. "But I…" What? Didn't want it? Couldn't imagine a life running The Ladder H? Hadn't asked her mother to make such a terrible decision? "Oh, Rosie," she moaned.

"Look at her!" Hugh glared at his daughter and then turned to Clinton. "She's a sniveling little–"

"That is quite enough." Clinton cut off Hugh's hateful words. "Speak with decorum, or I can have you removed," the attorney warned Hugh.

"Removed? How dare you?"

Bailey watched as her dad's face turned red, and perspiration glistened on his brow. She interrupted, "Clinton..." But the attorney looked at her dead in the eyes and shook his head no.

"Mr. Reynolds. I understand that this must be very frustrating for you, but I will repeat the last wishes of your late wife. The company is to be transferred to Mrs. Reynolds' sole heir, Bailey Ray Reynolds, to be managed in trust, facilitated through this firm, until she feels capable of accepting that responsibility. Should Ms. Reynolds be unable, or unwilling, to accept the role as head of The Ladder H Distilling Company, then her next of kin, Rosie Ann Moore, will inherit the entirety of Sherry's estate."

"I made this company!" Hugh's voice grated with rage. "I made you, Clinton."

Ethan got up from his chair to stand next to Hugh. "Rosie is a minor. She would need a guardian to care for her trust." His head bobbed on his neck as he nodded, and the words fell out of his mouth, faster and faster. "Look, clearly Bailey doesn't want this. We, Rosie's grandfather and I, can continue to care for The Ladder H—like we always have! We can teach Rosie and Bailey could visit, and—"

"No."

"Hear me out! Clinton, really—"

The attorney squared his shoulders and slightly lowered his head. Bailey could see his jacket stretch across his shoulders as he took a deep, calming breath. When he raised his chin to match his gaze with Ethan's, Clinton looked very much like the thousand-dollar-per-hour trial attorney Ethan had forgotten he was.

"Mr. Moore & Mr. Reynolds, thank you for your time. You are free to go. Bailey and I have a few last details to discuss, and you are no longer needed." Clinton walked to the door and opened it, allowing two men in dark suits to walk into the boardroom. "Gentleman, these men will escort you out."

Hugh followed Ethan out the door, but not before glaring at Clinton. "You'll hear from my attorney."

Bailey's eyes widened when Clinton laughed.

"I hope I do."

The mahogany table felt hard and cold against her forehead. Bailey could hear footsteps in the hall and the raspy scratch of Clinton's pants as he readjusted in his seat.

"Bailey."

"No."

"Bailey."

"I'm a mom. Don't talk to me like a child."

"Fine, can you please look at me?"

"No. The table is the only thing holding me up right now."

"I can see that." Clinton's small laugh turned into a choking cough. "You can do this, Ms. Reynolds."

She lifted her head and glared at him. "What if I don't want to?"

"Well, that would be a fine dilemma to put Rosie in..."

Her sapphire blue eyes hardened, and her voice lowered into a growl. "Don't make threats about my daughter. I didn't do this...Mama did."

"I don't need threats, Bailey. I've only ever told you the truth."

He wasn't lying. More than once, he'd had a hard truth for her, but she couldn't think of a time he'd ever lied to her. "Why?"

"Why did Sherry leave you The Ladder H?"

"Um, do you have other burning questions you think I need answered?"

"I don't think it's the wrong question, per se, but there are more interesting ones."

"Clint, don't you start with me," said Bailey, frustration causing her voice to purr with a little Texas twang.

"Listen, your mother set up her Last Will & Testament decades ago. She was clear from the very beginning that your father would never own The Ladder H."

"But—"

"Did she hope there would be more than one heir to carry the burden of running the family business? Yes...so very much so...yes. It turned out Rusty wasn't any better a father than he was a businessman. Sherry had already let him get to her family's company. She wasn't about to give him more children."

"She just...never once." Bailey stood up abruptly, pushing her chair back. "I never knew she was so unhappy."

"Sherry was an admirable woman. She wasn't a complainer." He ran his palm across the table's polished surface. "You were her joy. She used to call you her ray of sunshine. Every minute she had with you and Rosie...wait, I have something for you." Clinton stood up and walked to a dark wooden credenza along the boardroom's back wall. Out of his pocket, he drew a jangling set of keys to unlock the center top drawer. As he turned toward her, he reached out to hand her an old, worn envelope. "This is for you."

She was probably imagining the sweet smell of her mother's apricot-scented cold cream, but the rough paper of Mama's beloved monogrammed stationery was unmistakable. Sherry used the same linen paper for every thank-you note, letter to the principal, and RSVP she'd painstakingly inked over the years. Her perfect penmanship graced the ivory letterhead topped with Sherry's gold embossed initials.

"What's in it?"

"I'm not sure. She delivered it after her diagnosis."

"She loved handwritten letters." Bailey traced the inky black lines that spelled out her name on the front of the envelope. "She must have sent one to Rosie and me every day for the last year."

"She loved her granddaughter as much as she did you...I know she didn't want to hurt either of you."

Bailey looked at Clinton and then sat back down. She laid the envelope on the table in front of her.

"It's not that I'm hurt, Clinton...I'm scared."

"You?"

"I appreciate your confidence in me, but I messed it up before."

"You didn't mess up anything. At least not any more than any other typical, silly, twenty-something-year-old trying to figure out how to live their life."

"Rosie doesn't have a dad because of me."

He raised an eyebrow. "Really? That's the story you're

telling yourself?"

"It's the truth."

"Wouldn't hold up in court."

Bailey looked at him for a moment and then picked up her mother's letter. "Let's see what she thinks." A tear dripped down her cheek at the sound of the cream paper tearing. A moist droplet fell on the single piece of paper she pulled out of the envelope and, blurring the inky edges of her mother's familiar script.

Dearest Bailey,

Well, sunshine, if you're reading this...I think I owe you an apology. I know you'll be shaking your head no, but that's just hogwash. I never could figure out how to do this better. Sometimes I wondered if it would be easier if Rusty had the son he always wanted, but I couldn't imagine a life without you in it...and little Rosie. That girl is the spittin' image of you as a babe. Just as sweet as a freshly ripened Georgia peach. You two...you're my world.

And, because of that, I've made the choice I did. You deserve this, girl. It was always your heritage, and I let you run away from it...back home, where I wanted to be so badly, but you can't spend your life with your head in the horse trough. You'll need to be brave in a way I never could be. Clinton said he'd help you, hun' and I know he will, but your daddy has never been easy.

Baby girl, don't you let him push you around.

My heart is always with you,

Mama

"That's it?"

"What does it say?"

"She basically told me to suck it up!"

Clinton's laugh seemed out of place in the quiet room. "Ah, but that sounds just like Sherry."

Bailey folded up the letter and picked up the envelope to slip it back inside. "There's something else in here." She tipped the envelope upside down, and a key fell onto the table.

Clinton leaned forward. "She didn't mention that."

"No, she didn't." Picking it up, she spun the key in her hand. The numbers make me think it's a safe deposit box."

"Perhaps..."

"What am I going to do?"

"Well, fortunately, I've been working on a plan."

"I'm not going to like this, am I?"

"I've never known you to be happy about anything I've suggested before, but--"

"But I've never regretted it..."

"That's what I wanted to hear." Clinton's eyes lit up when he said, "Okay, so, here's what we need to do..."

Chapter Six

Bailey

"So, that's it."

"Wow, your mom really pulled an after death whammy, didn't she?"

"Yeah," Bailey said, before she pointed at the stainless-steel teapot resting on the farmhouse's old stove. "Don't put that in there. It doesn't work."

"Your teapot doesn't work?" Candice asked as she pivoted to find some other way to heat the mug of water in her hand.

"There was an incident. I may have put cocoa in there for Rosie and me. It did a bubble over thing, and I never figured out how to get it clean."

"I think you need something to counteract the bottle of wine you just poured into your stomach." Candice opened the cabinets and began digging through the old tea bags she found. "Chamomile could be good...and crepes. Yes, we can make you something light..."

Bailey swirled the bit of wine left in her glass. "Those croissants you make are amazing."

"They also take me twelve hours." She grabbed the glass from Bailey. "You need something a little faster than that."

"Can you believe she did this to me?"

Candice stopped putting a mug full of water in the microwave to turn towards Bailey. "What? Left you the heiress to a multi-million-dollar company, 200 acres of prime Texas land, and the Lord knows what else?"

"Yeah, that."

"Sure, it sounds awful." Candice bent to pull a bowl out of the cabinet by the stove.

"Well, you make it sound perfectly acceptable."

"Bailey, I know you're upset, but there are people who would kill for this."

"My dad would. His head about popped when Clint read off Mama's will." Bailey stood up, teetered a bit, and then walked to the fridge. Her fingers traced the edge of a small photo with her daughter's smiling face. "This was Rosie last year after her school Christmas play. Ethan has never seen her smile like that."

"Your dad and Ethan are missing out...and it's their fault, not yours."

"I did it all wrong, Candice."

"Aw, hun." The microwave dinged, and Candice pulled out the mug. "If you're guilty of anything, it's falling in love and hoping for the best. You need to fight. If not for you, then for that little girl." She pointed to the photo of Rosie on the fridge, dropped a bag of tea in the cup, and handed it to Bailey. "That's hot."

Bailey cradled the mug between her hands. "What's going on with the bank?"

Candice fumbled with the egg she was preparing to crack. "You're changing the subject."

"You're avoiding it," accused Bailey. "I'm worried about my friend, and I'd rather talk about your problems than mine."

"Sugar, our problems are nothing alike."

Bailey walked over to her friend, put down her tea, and removed the egg from her hand before placing it carefully back in the carton. "How bad is it?"

Candice braced herself against the counter. "I don't know yet, but I'll tell you next week. I'm meeting with an accountant on Monday."

"How much?"

"Enough…"

"Enough that…?"

"Yeah."

Bailey pulled her friend in for a hug. "We'll figure it out. Apparently, I'm rich, now."

Candice's laugh broke the sad ache that permeated the kitchen. "Girl, I hope it doesn't come to that."

"Nathan left you buried in debt. You can't learn to swim in a storm."

Candice shook her head. "Well, you aren't the only one who made poor choices with her ex."

Bailey slapped the counter and opened her mouth, but the doorbell interrupted her tipsy tirade. "Who's that?"

"It's your house. I don't know."

Bailey rolled her eyes and walked through the living room

to the front door. Framed by the door's sheer curtains, a pair of familiar eyes met hers through the window glass. "You've got to be kidding me."

Chapter Seven

Mac

What the hell was he thinking? He knew better. The second his editor pushed that morning's copy of the New York Times in front of him, he put two and two together and felt like a fool.

"Her?"

"Yeah, I know, you don't do the celebrity gossip pieces, but this is BIG."

"James, no," Mac said as he saw Bailey's sweet, smiling eyes. When he returned to O'Toole's and she was gone…he'd thought it was the last time he'd ever see those soft lashes flutter down to those pink cheeks. The last time she would tilt her chin up to him and smile. He wanted her to stay, but he could guess why she had disappeared that night.

It could have been the burning tension between them…too hot. Maybe he scared her off. It could have been his ridiculous friends. He'd given her too much time to think between soft touches. Whatever it had been, he had to admit he'd hoped he'd see her again. Like this, though? In a gritty, black and white sheet of newsprint?

"Oh, yes, Mac. This is what you need to do to get off of war crimes and battles over blood diamonds. The Ladder H legacy is getting all the headlines. It's just baby steps away from presidential scandals and global power plays. You could be New York's most 'in-the-know' journalist."

"But—"

"No. Mac, you're running out of options. You said you won't go back into the field. If nothing else, our insurance won't cover it after that incident in Uzbekistan."

"Hey, my therapist cleared me to return to work."

James picked up a pencil from his desk. He watched it as it spun between his fingers. "Mac, it's this or nothing. I think you need this and, honestly, I need you."

"Come on, James, it's a puff piece!"

"Ms. Reynolds is notoriously cagey. She hasn't given the media an interview in years. After her divorce, she moved off to Texas and has been hiding there ever since."

Mac thought about those soft curls falling around her face and the hurt in her eyes when she said I'm divorced. He'd had no clue how complicated that one statement had been. "James."

"Mac." James laid the pencil back down on the desk.

Its sharp point directed Mac's eyes to her face on the grayed paper of the front page. He wanted to see the spunky twist in her smile again. "What exactly are you asking for here?"

"The story that nobody else is getting! That's what I want. Why did her mother give The Ladder H to Ms. Reynolds? I want to know why Hugh Reynolds is suing his own daughter."

"You've always been greedy."

James smiled. "It's not greed. It's curiosity."

"I can't promise all that, but I will talk to her." Mac shook his head gently from side to side. "I have a few questions I'd like to ask her myself."

He'd begun imagining her reaction at five thousand feet. Through the plane's small portal windows, he watched the golden hills of Texas roll out below him. The businessman next to him was shuffling papers and ogling the flight attendant whenever she passed their row with her cart. The guy tried to give him the bro code wink at one point, and Mac turned his head to look outside.

Bailey was making his stomach twist. He'd traveled thousands of miles knowing that he was heading into a guaranteed conflict. At best, he'd look like a stalker, and, at worst, he'd be enemy number one—the press. For her type, there wasn't a lower life form. The rich elite paid a premium for their privacy and gold-plated lifestyle. His type revealed their shortcomings and aired out their dirty laundry in public...all for view rates and subscription sales. He was basically a parasite.

Mac had never wanted it to be that way. When he started out as a journalist, he bragged about his high morals and incorruptible ethics. His work was saving the world by uncovering one political scandal after another. He was taking down the bad guys...until he wasn't. The media had changed. Readers didn't want news; they wanted gossip. It took some time to notice the difference.

He'd ended up as a journalist because of his father. The man who raised Mac had been distant and strict, but he made sure Mac had everything he needed. The only softness he saw as a boy was his summers with his Nana. Tour after tour, he followed his father from one corner of the globe to another. He saw his dad play the diplomat and noble protector, but the game of war had never appealed to Mac. He wanted to help people, not kill them. When given the choice to enlist or go to school, he chose a career in journalism.

Now, instead of heading to another country, he was heading to her hometown. He was going to breach her safe place, her haven, to bring the wolves to her door. He wanted an excuse to see her, but damned if James hadn't hung his ass out on the line.

"Ladies and gentlemen, welcome to Houston. Local time is 12:13 p.m. and the temperature is 93 degrees. For your safety and comfort, please remain seated with your seat belt fastened until the captain turns off the fasten seat belt sign."

He was going to need to figure out a way to spin this...a way to get a second chance, while also keeping his job, and he was going to need to do it fast.

Chapter Eight

Mac

The wooden steps of the old farmhouse creaked under Mac's feet. He could see sheer white curtains through the square windows of her front door. The entire farm looked like a movie set. There was a barn painted burnt umber off to his left, and the house had gray, faded wood peeking out behind chipping white paint. The sound of a lone cow's moo traveled from somewhere nearby. An old blue pickup was sitting on a weedy gravel driveway. The oppressive Texas heat made it hard for him to breathe, and his chest was tightening with fear. "Please, Lord, don't let her shoot me."

His knuckles tapped the door three times, and he took a step back to wait. Mac was counting his breaths and using his field training to stay calm. She wasn't coming. Would he have to come back later to relive this moment again? Her voice, faint and angry, rang out in the house, and he could hear her footsteps approaching the door.

Mac smiled when her face showed up, framed in the glass.

He took a step forward when she opened the door. "Hello—"

"What are you doing here?" Bailey put one hand on the door frame and the other on her hip.

"Bailey, I know this is a little weird." Mac shoved his hands in his pockets. "I—"

"Have no reason to be here? Was not invited? Don't have any darned clue how to take a hint?"

"Well, sort of...see...I saw you in the paper." Mac could tell from the look on her face that that was the wrong thing to say.

"Oh? So, you thought you'd stalk the grieving heiress? What do you think you're going to get from me?"

"I'm sorry, Bailey, I didn't mean it that way," he said, waving his arm around. "When I came back to the bar, yeah, I was disappointed you weren't there, but this isn't what you think it is," he explained.

"No, Mac, I'm sorry." Bailey's eyes narrowed. "What do I think this is?"

"I'm not a dude you met in a New York bar that followed you to Texas."

"Sure, looks like that from where I'm standing."

"No, really, Bailey. The reason I am here is for work. I mean, I wanted to be here, but I know I didn't have any right to come find you. However, my boss asked me to be here. I thought it could be a good chance..."

"Asked, Mac?"

He was fucking this up so badly, and he knew it, but it was like a train wreck he couldn't stop. The momentum was already pulling him to his doom. "My boss, at the New York Times, he was hoping—"

"New York Times?" Bailey placed both of her hands on her hips. "Yes, Mac?"

"Look, he's just hoping for a story. I can help! Here, please, take my card." He shoved it towards her. "We can decide on what you feel comfortable sharing. We could—"

The slamming door pushed a gust of dry air and sandy grit towards his face, and his card fluttered to the ground. He could hear her yelling inside. Mac couldn't make out what she was saying, but when the door cracked open and he was looking down the double barrel of a well-cared-for shotgun.

He backed down the stairs slowly and wondered if he'd ever had a chance of this going well. It wasn't until his foot hit the gravel driveway that the gun barrel disappeared, and the door slammed shut. "Fuck."

Mac was getting ready to climb into the sensible four-door sedan that the paper rented for him when he heard a holler from the barn.

"Hello?" It was clear someone was yelling, but he couldn't understand what they were saying. He slammed the car door and started walking towards the barn. As he grew closer, the muffled cries sounded more like angry curses, then they stopped. "Hey, can I help?"

"Get out of here!" The words erupted from the barn as Mac opened the wide red doors.

"Man, I'm sorry. I thought you needed help." As he backed away, Mac's eyes landed on a man trapped under a large piece of wood in the corner. A goat was nibbling on his hair.

"Get off me, you trash can with hooves!" The man saw Mac and tried to push away the wood pressing down on his chest. "Thank goodness. Can you help me?"

Mac rushed forward. "Yeah, let me—" He grunted and pulled at a piece of timber. The trapped man moaned as the wood lifted off his chest. "Can you slide out?"

"Yeah, but there's something grabbing me."

"Hey, stop!" Mac cried as a goat bit his foot and tried to eat his shoelaces. The wood shifted in his hand as he kicked the hairy menace away.

"Watch it!" the man shouted, while Mac tried to steady his hold on the wood. There was a small bloom of scarlet forming on the man's blue plaid shirt.

"I can't hold it much longer. I'm going to lift it as high as I can, then you've got to move!"

The man shoved at the goat and half-rolled, half-pushed out from under the beam. The goat gave a loud bleat and clopped away into the dark barn as the beam hit the ground with a thud and a bounce.

"Are you okay?" Mac leaned down and patted the man on the ground, trying to see where the blood was coming from.

"Yeah, I think a nail caught me." The man was trying to sit up when the barn door flew open wide.

"What the heck is going on in here?"

"Aw, Bailey, I'm so sorry. Rosie's goat —"

Bailey rushed to kneel next to the man on the ground. Mac stepped back and stared at them awkwardly. Who was this guy? He didn't want to think about those thick arms wrapped around her.

"Jackson, you fool! I told you not to hoist that beam alone."

"Well, I could have done it if that deranged goat hadn't taken a bite out of my bum while I was trying to step up on the ladder."

Bailey cursed under her breath and looked in the direction Captain Sparkle Pants had disappeared. "He is a darned tyrant, but Rosie loves him." She patted Jackson's shirt and felt the slight snag where blood soaked into the fabric. Bailey turned to Mac and said, "Thank you...who knows what would have happened if—"

Mac shook his head and grabbed Jackson's hand to help pull him off the floor. "Let's not fill in the blanks with things that didn't happen." Mac patted Jackson's back. "You okay, man?"

"I am, thanks to you." Jackson reached out to shake Mac's hand. "Can I ask who you are?"

Bailey's face paled in the dark shadows of the barn. "Well, it doesn't matter. He's just about to leave."

"Well, now..." Mac started, but the look in Bailey's eyes caused him to pause. "Yeah, I stopped by to...check...on Ms. Reynolds. After I heard the news of her loss, I worried about her."

"You were, huh?" Jackson asked as he slid a thumb through a belt loop and adjusted his stance.

"We're...close friends."

Bailey rolled her eyes. "I wouldn't say close. Hell, I wouldn't say friends."

Mac turned his gaze to meet her blue eyes. "I don't know,

Bailey. We were pretty close."

"Well, I think I need to have this scrape looked at." Jackson cleared his throat and shifted towards the door. "Mr. Mac, let me know if you need help figuring out how to get home." He gave Bailey a pointed stare, and then he walked away.

"Mac, now you've gone and given Jackson thoughts he has no right to be thinking."

"Bailey, I've been thinking those thoughts all day."

She looked down at the ground where the beam lay, and a small smear of blood painted the wood red. Her shoulders softened. "Thank you for helping him."

Mac reached his hand out to touch her, and she stepped back. "Bailey."

"No, Mac. I can't."

"Can't what? Trust me?"

Bailey shook her head, then lifted her chin. "I appreciate your help. Jackson does, too, but I think it's time for you to leave."

"Mama? Whose car is that?" Rosie's voice traveled from the front steps.

Bailey's gaze flew to the door. "I don't want her to see you."

"You can't build walls forever. You can't hide."

"We'll see."

The old barn door creaked as she pulled it closed a bit before she hollered, "Rosie, hun, I'm headed in...go on and finish getting ready for bed." Bailey slipped through the crack left in the door. "Goodbye, Mac," she sighed, before she left him alone in the growing darkness.

Chapter Nine

Bailey

"Then what happened?" asked Rosie, while wiggling in her bed.

"Mr. Jackson went to see Dr. Jess and the newsman from New York left."

"Did Dr. Jess fix him? Will Jackson be okay? Why was the New York man here?"

Bailey tucked the lacy lavender blanket up under Rosie's chin before leaning down to leave a soft kiss on her forehead. "You ask a lot of questions."

"Silly mom. You told me there are no bad questions."

Bailey laughed as she reached over to the small crystal and pink-tasseled lamp on the nightstand. "They aren't bad! There are just too many!" she said, as she pulled the cord on the window blinds and the room went dark. Bailey leaned down to whisper in her daughter's ear. The little girl's soft blonde hair tickled her cheek, and Bailey took a deep breath before whispering. "How much do I love you?"

Rosie's giggle filled the dark room. "So much."

"So much, baby." With one last kiss on Rosie's forehead, Bailey said goodnight and stepped out into the hallway, closing the door behind her.

A sigh slipped through her lips. "Mac, why'd you have to show up here?"

As Bailey walked through the dark house, checking door locks and closing windows for the night, the lull of a quiet Texas evening pressed in on her. It had been the hardest part of leaving New York. Without the constant sounds of people moving around her, she felt so alone. Wide open plains were good for finding your own space and building a home, but the loneliness was a constant companion. Raising her daughter as a single mom was one of the hardest and most satisfying things she'd ever done. Despite the hardships she experienced when she left New York and moved back to her family's Texas home, she knew what safety felt like. Sherry had always protected her, and Bailey had been selfish. Raised with everything a young girl could ask for, it took Bailey too much time to really appreciate her life. She hadn't understood the lessons her mother tried to teach her until there'd been nothing left of her old life.

Even then, she knew that her "nothing" had been so much more than other people's nothing. What was Candice going to do with the bakery? Something had to change. Bailey and the folks in town wouldn't let anything happen to Patty Cakes, the cute little shop that Candice's mother opened almost twenty years ago.

Bailey couldn't have survived in Texas without Candice's help. Her friend knew what it was like to live alone, to lose her mother bit by bit to a debilitating medical condition, and to grow up without a father. They'd been two young women who found their way in the world together. They would find their way through this, too.

She asked the silence, "Mom, what the heck were you thinking?" Bailey didn't really need an answer, though. She already knew. Sherry had grit. She might have had patience for days, but when things were hard, Sherry dug in her heels and tucked her chin down like a horse headed home.

Bailey wasn't ready to head north to New York. Their house in the city hadn't felt like her home in a very long time.

Clinton's legal strategy started with her moving back. He wanted her in the city long enough to sort out her mom's estate and set up a management team for The Ladder H. That would prove Bailey deserved the gift her mother gave her and that she could manage the company as well. Then Bailey would have to deal with Hugh and Ethan.

After Bailey checked the lock on the front door, she peeked into Rosie's room. For a moment, she listened in the darkroom to her daughter's soft, rhythmic breathing. Whatever she did, she would not hurt that little girl. There were parts of New York that Rosie would love...Central Park, the Rockettes, the lights in Times Square, and the history of Liberty Island. She'd want ice cream in the park, and they'd have proper snow in the winter. She and Rosie could go to the Macy's Thanksgiving Day parade.

Maybe...she and Mac could go on an actual date. They could have a romantic dinner or take a carriage ride and end the evening at O'Toole's bar. "Rein it in, Bailey." She cautiously let her mind wander while she pulled on pajamas and brushed her teeth. As her head hit the pillow, full of what-ifs and maybes for a life in New York, she heard Captain Sparkle Pants bleat out a cry in the barn, followed by the restless neigh of Rosie's pony, Princess Star. "Tomorrow. There's time to figure it out tomorrow."

Chapter Ten

Mac

This was Mac's last chance to convince Bailey he was in Texas for more than a story. That morning, the desk clerk at his hotel told him everyone in town would be at the Fourth of July picnic. He imagined gingham tablecloths and the mayor in a dunk tank. There would be kids laughing around the carnival games, and moms would exhaust themselves trying to clean cotton candy off small sticky faces.

It wasn't the long flights, the sleepless nights surrounded by grown men crying in their sleep, or the hatred he'd seen in a stranger's eyes that forced him out of war correspondence. It was the small limp bodies covered in dust as the last echoes of an explosive boom reverberated through far-off alleys he couldn't forget.

As he walked through the small town of Serenity, he admired the old, whitewashed buildings with their shiplap siding and the small pots of flowers resting in front of every store. The tinkling music of an ice cream truck and kids' laughter led him to the grassy town square. In the center, a freshly painted white gazebo was covered in red, white, and blue crepe paper mums and flowing streamers. "Where are you, Bailey?" he mumbled to himself. Looking around, he watched as women sashayed by him in sun dresses and smiles, but none of them were her.

How the hell was he supposed to know that his life would change that night when he walked into O'Toole's? He'd gone from wondering how many drinks it would take to forget his day to hoping for a single kiss that would clear away all the thoughts in his whirling brain.

"I'd have thought you'd be north of the Mason-Dixon line by now."

Mac turned to find Jackson grinning from ear to ear under a tan cowboy hat. "It looks like you're recovering well after your run-in with Captain Rainbow Furry Sparkle Pants."

Jackson patted his shoulder. "I owe you a thank you. If you hadn't shown up, it would have been a lot worse than just another scar to impress the ladies."

"You'll need to come up with a better story than 'a little girl's goat tried to kill me.'"

"Yeah," said Jackson. "But that's one mean goat!"

A soft, familiar voice said, "Aw, he's a softy. You just need to know how to reach his little goat heart."

Mac's shoulders jerked when he heard Bailey's voice. He pulled his face into a mask of indifference when he saw Jackson's crooked smile, and turned towards her voice before asking, "And how would one do that?"

"Food," said Bailey, and winked. "For men, it's always food."

Jackson nodded and said, "She's not wrong!" He pointed to the picnic tables on the far side of the park. "Ms. Sally brought her famous pecan pie. I think I need to grab a piece before it's all gone." He winked at Bailey before he walked off, "But don't you dare tell Candice! She's been trying to best Ms. Sally's pie recipe for years."

Bailey feigned shock and hollered, "Jackson, how could you?"

He tossed a last look over his shoulder and shrugged. "I like pie!"

"It is good pie." Bailey smiled up at Mac.

"Should we get some before it's gone?" He asked, his voice dropping low.

"Nah," said Bailey. "Candice would kill me!"

Mac shook his head. "We wouldn't want that..."

"Mac, what are you doing here?"

"I wasn't ready to leave Serenity." He looked around the park. "It might be growing on me."

"Really? You're not still hoping to get a story?"

"Bailey..."

"I know. Someone is going to write that story." She shook her head and glared at him. "It doesn't matter if I give them my side or not."

Mac raised his hand and then let it drop to his side. "You deserve your privacy, Bailey. Mourning your mom's death should be all you're focused on now, but you know that's not how this works." He knew he was pushing her, but he also knew the extreme lengths his fellow journalists would go for a good story.

"I gave up my privacy when I showed up in New York

for mom's funeral." Bailey turned to a group of laughing kids surrounded by a cloud of bubbles. "Rosie didn't consent to having her life picked apart any more than I did."

He looked at the wrinkles between her eyebrows. The tension in her shoulders made him ache. He wanted to pull her close and run his hands down her arms to stroke the anxiety away. "You could give it all up and sink back into anonymity." He shook his head as the words left his mouth. That wouldn't fix their problems. He needed the story...he needed her to be happy.

"My mother would turn in her grave," said Bailey. Her voice dripped sadness, but she stood in front of him like she was preparing for war.

Mac raised an eyebrow and said, "You don't want to disappoint her."

Bailey paused, took a breath, then lifted her chin to look up into Mac's eyes. "I was thinking about you."

"Yeah?" a smile twisted the edge of his lips. "You thinking about that night?"

"No. I was thinking about last night."

"Jackson seems like he's doing fine."

"Mac—"

"Mom!" Rosie yelled before barreling into her mom's side. "Mom? Mom. Mom!"

Bailey wrapped her arm around Rosie and pulled her close for a long squeeze while her daughter squirmed. "Girl! What's gotten into you?"

"They're about to do the three-legged race!" Rosie grabbed Bailey's hand and pulled her towards the crowd forming by the small roped-off area near the gazebo.

"But—"

Mac laughed. "She knows what she wants."

Bailey glanced at Mac over her daughter's head. "Just because she wants it doesn't mean she should have it."

"What's the harm?"

"Hun, stop." Bailey stood her ground as her daughter tried to pull her off her feet. "I can't do the three-legged race."

Rosie looked up at Bailey and Mac before asking, "No! Why not?"

"I'm so sorry, Candice asked me to watch her booth. She's having a little trouble getting help at the bakery right now. I offered to help her."

"You said I could do the race when I was big enough! I really wanted to try this year."

Mac watched the mother and daughter debate. Rosie had some good points, but Bailey was determined to keep her promise to her friend. He asked, "Can I help?"

Bailey looked at him with surprise. "Really?"

"Sure," said Mac with a shrug.

Rosie started jumping up and down. "Yes! Please, Mom!"

Bailey dropped to her knees. "Rosie, you just met Mac. It wouldn't be nice to ask him to change his plans for you."

Mac watched Bailey closely. "I offered. Rosie didn't ask."

"See, Mom! Mac says he'd like to take me to the race." Rosie let go of her mom's hand and snatched his hand instead.

He looked down into her eyes, and he squeezed her hand gently to stop his from shaking. The little girl looked up at him with eyes filled with hope and trust. He'd seen that look before in the eyes of moms and children as they begged him to make them feel safe again. Mac pushed a yes past the knot in his throat.

Rosie smiled up at Mac and then looked at her mom. "See?"

"Are you sure?" Bailey asked Mac.

"It's a three-legged race," he said, but he wasn't sure if he was comforting her or himself. "What could happen? Do you trust me?"

Bailey whispered, "I don't know yet."

"I wish you would." Mac glanced down at Rosie. Her attention drifted back to the other kids on the grassy field. "Have I given you a reason not to?"

"Not yet."

"Well, if you can't come up with a good reason, then I guess you should give it a try." Mac smiled and shrugged.

As Rosie ran off to join the other kids picking up their sacks, Mac turned around to smile at Bailey. As he walked away, he could have sworn she whispered, "I just might."

Mac glanced across the field to where Bailey was moving pastries around a long table inside a ruffled-covered booth, and then he looked down at Rosie as she smiled up at him. "How does this work? You're like two feet tall, and I am six foot three."

"Have you ever done a three-legged race before?"

"At my age, I really thought there weren't a lot of firsts left for me, kid. Seems like you found one."

"Oh!" Rosie giggled and said, "You're going to love it! I've never done it before, either. I watch every year, though! They look like giant monsters running across the finish line!"

She grabbed his hand and led him over to the check-in table for the three-legged race. An older woman smiled at him with gray hair curls bouncing in the soft breeze. "Oh, hello," she said, "Miss Rosie, who is your handsome partner?"

"Hi, Mrs. Grace, this is my mom's friend from New York!"

"New York?" she said, as she glanced at Mac. He could see the curiosity buzzing in her eyes. Her lips parted, and then she closed her mouth. "Interesting"

Mac gave her a crooked smile and shrugged. "I'm here for pie and the three-legged race." He cocked his shoulder and thumbed in Rosie's direction. "I couldn't disappoint her, could I?"

"No!" Rosie laughed.

As Mac collected the burlap sack and said thank you, he glanced around at the people preparing for the race. Moms in dresses hobbled around with one leg stuck in a sack while their children looped their arms around their thighs. A few couples were braving the race. One was fighting, and another was hip-to-hip when they paused for a quick kiss and a laugh at the starting line.

Rosie pulled on his hand and said, "Are you ready, Mac?"

"We're gonna need a strategy...I suspect that couple over smooching will be the fastest. They have the longest legs, the smallest handicap, and they seem to be aligned as a team."

Rosie squished her eyebrows into a serious face. "Hm, I think you're right."

"Ok, soldier. We're going to divert and tackle."

Rosie tapped his hip and glanced sideways at the contestants near them. "Mac, we can't hit them."

"Tackle the problem." Mac rubbed the scrabble on his chin as he watched the other people practicing. "Okay, give me the sack." As Rosie handed him the sack, he helped her lift her foot and slide her leg inside. Then he followed with his own. "Hold on to my thigh tight."

Rosie shook her head and said, "Okay."

Mac lifted his leg, and Rosie giggled as she flew into the air. "It's like an elevator!"

"It's more like a lift," said Mac, as he bounced her up and down a few times. "Well, swing your leg so it looks like you're doing something, but otherwise focus on holding on tight."

"Yes, sir!"

Mac paused and looked down at the blonde-haired little girl as she wiggled like a salmon next to him. He'd seen children happy, of course, but this was something else. There was a sense of awe and wonder in her eyes that he hadn't seen in a long time. Instead of figuring out how to live, he'd been fighting against injustice. He'd forgotten how to stop and play...it awoke an ache in his gut. He'd considered a family over the years, but it never seemed like the right time, the right woman, the right place. Mac's mind wandered through the possibilities.

A whistle snapped him from his contemplation, and Rosie pulled on his shirt and asked, "Are you ready?"

"I guess I'd better be." His lips parted in a wry smile, and he patted her back as he waddled to the starting line with her clinging to his side.

Rosie practically vibrated next to him as the officiant read off the rules and reminded everyone to play fair.

"Get ready," Max said as he wrapped his arm around her upper body and held her securely. The second the starting gun went off, his leg started pumping. He could feel her bounce up as he shifted his foot, and her laughter was contagious. She belted out belly laughs every time he lifted his leg to step forward, and she flew in the air over and over again. They laughed their way across the field as she held onto him for dear life.

"Quick Mac! They're right behind us!"

He tucked his chin to brace himself to run faster. Her laughter fueled him to push himself as fast as he could while they raced closer and closer to the finish line. As the plastic tape hit his chest, he stumbled, and he fell onto the field. Mac twisted to avoid crushing Rosie, and he fell on his back with her, laughing in his ear. They tumbled and rolled across the lawn as the other runners ran past them, some of them falling into the soft blades of grass as well.

He glanced over and saw her smiling in the sunshine. She looked like a young, carefree version of her mother. Her eyes and her nose matched perfectly, though he didn't know where the blonde hair came from.

"We won!" Rosie screamed.

"Nice work, partner," said Mac as he pushed himself up off the ground and reached down to lift her upright.

The race official came by and put a blue ribbon necklace around Rosie's neck. A shiny, plastic metal sign that read 'First Place' dangled off it. "Let's go show mom!"

Mac grinned and said, "You lead, I'll follow."

Chapter Eleven

Bailey

The sun had set an hour before. Mac and Rosie had spent the whole day watching the parade, eating pie, and trying to win the carnival games. When Bailey could step away from her friend's booth, she joined them. "I don't remember the last time I've had so much fun," she said, as she stroked her daughter's soft blonde curls and readjusted the small gold trophy tucked under Rosie's armpit. "I also don't remember the last time I ate so much!"

They'd settled down on a quilt in the grass after eating hot dogs and strawberry shortcake. Other families joined them, each on their own blanket island, ready to watch the evening fireworks. Exhausted, Rosie lay her head down on Bailey's lap and fell asleep, almost immediately, while listening to the family surrounding them.

Mac watched Bailey in the dimming light. The rays of the setting sun softened her skin and showed the early hints of laugh lines at the corners of her eyes. He wondered if his mom would've looked like that...tired from chasing him, but radiant, with all that love glowing from within. He admired Bailey. Life gave her both blessings and curses, and she'd done her best with both. She had privileges neither he nor his friends enjoyed, but she was also perfectly happy without them.

"I had a really nice time today. Thank you for letting me spend the day with you and Rosie."

"After seeing you dance, I'm impressed by how well you managed running in a bag."

Mac arched an eyebrow and broke out his cheesiest Texas drawl. "Are you knockin' my two-step?"

"Perhaps," said Bailey, before she laughed and pointed into the sky.

He looked up as the first blossoming firework lit the sky, then fell towards them with a gentle crackle. "Bailey, I know you have no reason to trust me, but I hope you will."

"You can't—"

"I didn't know it was you when we met at the bar that night," he interrupted her. His voice dropped to a quiet whisper. She almost couldn't hear him over the fireworks. "I'm so glad you were there."

Bailey's eyes widened as Mac tentatively reached out, his palm gently coming to rest on her thigh. She felt a spark at his touch, her gaze flickering to Rosie before returning to Mac's hand, her breath catching slightly. The warmth of his palm seeped through the denim of her jeans, sending a shiver up her spine. Mac's fingers were long, his touch gentle yet confident, and she could feel her muscles tense beneath his caress. Her gaze lifted to meet his, her eyes filled with a mixture of curiosity and caution, a silent conversation passing between them.

"What are you doing, Mac?" she asked softly, her voice barely a whisper, yet carrying a weight that hung in the air. Her heart pounded in her chest, her senses heightened, as she took in the scent of his cologne, a subtle mix of wood and spice that was uniquely him.

He leaned in closer, close enough for her to see the flecks of gold in his brown eyes, close enough for her to feel his breath on her cheek. "Has it been that long?" he murmured, his voice low and intimate, sending a wave of heat coursing through her. "Am I doing it wrong?" His fingers gently caressed her thigh, feeling the warmth radiating from her body, each touch sending a jolt of electricity straight to her core.

Bailey's cheeks flushed slightly, and she swallowed hard, her mouth suddenly dry. "No, but if I'm gonna give you the story, we can't mix business with pleasure. My mama taught me that," she said, her voice trembling slightly, betraying the tempest of emotions raging within her. She wanted to lean into his touch, to give in to the desire that was building inside her, but duty and propriety held her back.

He nodded his head once and slid his hand off her thigh. Instead, he reached towards his jacket lying nearby on the ground. "You look cold."

"No...just a little surprised."

"You've been through a lot, Bailey. I want to share that story with the world."

"The one where I left my husband because he used me? The one where my father yelled at me almost every day? The one where I abandoned my mother and left her in New York to handle both of them because I was too afraid to take care of it myself?"

"No, the one where you took your daughter to safety. The one where you built a new life here in Texas. The one where you are picking up the mantle of your mother's family business because you lived a life that earned her respect and pride."

"That's not my story."

"That's how I see it. Those different stories may be two sides of the same coin, but you don't have to keep trying to fit it into the same hole your dad and that guy kept trying to fit you into."

"It's so easy for you to say that. I couldn't tell my dad to stop. I couldn't ask my husband for more. Worse, I can't tell my mom I'm sorry. But I can show up, every day I can put a meal on the table for that kid. Every day I can put a smile on my face, so she knows nothing other than joy. When I went to New York, that all came crashing down."

This time Mac reached out and laid his hand laying gently on her cheek. "Bailey, you didn't do anything wrong."

"I saw Ethan there. Did you know Rosie has the same emerald green eyes? Sometimes I look at her and I see her father. I can't help but love him still in those moments because he gave me her, but reality hits, and I realize that sometimes I hate looking at her eyes because it reminds me of every minute I had to look at his...while he yelled at me, while he hurt me, and while I had to fight to leave. I didn't just break open the doors of that golden cage. I blew it up and left the whole darned thing heaped up in a mangled pile."

"Do you want to share your story with me?" Mac asked, then ran his hand across the scruff on his face. "Off the record."

Bailey looked at him. The celebratory fireworks were bursting over his head in the distance. There were shades of red, blues, and vivid purple. Each exploded and popped before falling from the sky. Despite the years since she fled to her little home in Texas, she didn't feel free. It hadn't been the independence she sought when she left Ethan. She's been looking for safety. Did she feel safe now?

Her house gave her a sturdy roof over her head; her community wrapped its arms around her, and she never felt alone; and Rosie, well, that little girl gave her more purpose and joy than she'd ever imagined was possible. Was she still trapped by her past?

In that moment, Mac's arms looked like safety...strong and sturdy. While she was still deciding how much she could trust him, she didn't think he would intentionally hurt her.

"It was a Wednesday night. There really wasn't anything special about it, but it's easy to remember because Rosie's birthday was the next day. I spent the day picking up her cake, balloons, and the last of the party favors. It had been three whole years since she flipped my world upside down. She was so excited! I mean, she probably didn't have a clue that it was her birthday, but she knew there was going to be a party."

Bailey smiled and ran a finger over her sleeping daughter's temple before tucking a tendril of hair behind her ear. "He wasn't home. Ethan had been working late every night. He said it was for some sort of tax audit at the same time as a launch for a new luxury line. Investors to schmooze and IRS agents to argue with, it felt, mostly, normal. It's just...he had never put in that much time at the office before."

Bailey raised her hand when Mac opened his mouth. "It's not that simple. Sure, he was probably having an affair, but I can't say I even cared about that. By then, it had been months since he'd touched me, and even longer since he'd said that precious four-letter word. We were falling apart, and I didn't even know why."

"Rosie was asleep. He came home. I was still decorating for the party. He smelled like booze and was weak on his feet." Bailey waved her hand towards the islands of laughing friends and family. "My whole life has been about the business. I don't think about drinking much, but getting piss drunk the night before your kid's birthday party?" Bailey shook her head.

"It happened really fast. I said something he took offense to and...well, it had never happened before, but I'll never forget the sound my teeth made when they cracked against each other, and the burn in my cheek lasted for two days."

"Oh, Bailey."

"It wasn't how I was raised. New Yorkers and Texans have at least one thing in common, and that's their intolerance for bullshit."

Mac laughed, then glanced quickly down at Rosie.

"He went to bed, and I packed my things. I waited until the car was ready and I woke up my baby and we went to mom's apartment in the city. The hardest part was taking that little sleeping girl out of her bed at 3 a.m. and knowing she would never lay her head back down on that pillow ever again.

"When I think back on that night, sometimes I smile when

I imagine him waking up to an empty house. Maybe he waited a couple of hours thinking I was running birthday errands. He sent so many texts. There were just as many missed calls. At some point, the guests would have arrived. What did he tell them? He stopped texting me in the afternoon. All communication after that was through the attorneys. That day we met at the bar was the first time I'd heard his voice since that night. Clinton, for being a thorn in my side, did an amazing job of keeping me out of that courtroom."

Mac shifted on the picnic blanket and started to say, "I'm—"

"No. I don't want sympathy. He got what he deserved, and I'd have had a thousand of those Wednesday nights if it meant Rosie would blossom into the bold, bright girl she is becoming."

"Grit, Bailey. That's what you got and loads of it."

"It's heavy to carry. I don't want any more grit." Bailey looked up at the quiet sky. The fireworks had ended during her story, and the townsfolk were packing up and disappearing into the night. "Have you felt that, Mac? Have you been in love?"

Mac thought about the last time he'd felt this way about a woman. Marisela had also been a fighter. "Yes." He answered Bailey's question, paused, then said, "Once before. It wasn't like this...it didn't last." He didn't want to say it hadn't gone well or that it hadn't ended well. Neither of those things were true.

"This?"

"We have something. You can't deny that."

"Tell me more about when you were in love."

"When I was in college, I took a summer to travel abroad. It was hard for me to stay in one place after moving constantly growing up. I needed a break from New York. I had some friends who were stationed near a small town in Spain, Puerto de Santa Maria. They were enlisted, but I was free to look around when they couldn't leave the base.

"While exploring the city, I met a young boy, Luis. I asked him where I would find the best lunch in town, and he led me to the local cantina where his mother worked. First, I fell for the food, then I fell for the kid, and then I fell for his mother. I would go there every day with or without my friends."

"She sounds exotic and beautiful."

"Yes, I guess she was those things, but she was also stubborn and a hard worker."

"Are you telling me you have a type?"

"Maybe." Mac laughed. "I visited every day to teach Luis how to speak English. At first, it gave me an excuse to keep going back, but then it felt like my life's purpose. Summer was ending, and I didn't want to go back home."

"Don't you know the first rule of a summer crush?"

"I guess I learned the hard way." Mac's voice whispered in the cooling night. "I showed up on a Tuesday. It was ten days before I was due to head home. I wanted to tell her I was going to stay so we could plan our future."

"It didn't go well?"

"She wasn't there. Not Tuesday, or Wednesday, or Thursday. I kept going back until the bartender took pity on me. He told me Marisela quit and wouldn't be coming back. To this day,

I don't know why. Was it me? Did she go back to Luis's dad? Was the bartender just lying?"

"Oh, Mac." Bailey reached out to place her hand on his knee in the dark. "It wasn't fair of her to leave without saying goodbye."

"I've thought about going back. Just to see if she was still there, but I don't want to do that." Mac reached out to run his fingers across the back of her hand. "I don't want to feel love like that."

"Love is hard." Bailey looked up at the stars in the sky. "It's also beautiful and complicated. I know it's not scarce...it was all around you today. In your friends in New York, and in your community. I am so glad I found that here in Serenity. I hope you find what you're looking for, too."

"I'm open to the possibilities."

Bailey and Mac sat in silence. The soft sound of Rosie's breathing blended with the chirping of the cicada and the distant hum of cars heading home.

"Mac, I don't want to do this."

He reached out to her but paused. His hand dropped to Rosie's head, and then he pulled it back. "You'll do it for her. The courts, the papers, the endless questions from people. None of it matters more than her."

"I might need you to keep telling me that." Bailey whispered into the night.

Chapter Twelve

Mac

Yes, he'd said off the record. Yes, he knew she'd be upset. Yes, she probably even had grounds to sue him and make his life ridiculously uncomfortable. The paper in front of him made his gut twist. Today's headline read, Texas Cowgirl returns as New York Socialite to Ruin Family's Fortune.

James let this run. Was he trying to force Mac's hand? Did he just want headlines and subscriptions? Mac didn't recognize the author but knew it would only take him a few minutes to hunt him down.

"Breathe, man. Murder won't help her," Mac mumbled to himself.

What he needed to do was tell Bailey's story. People needed to know that she was the victim. Lord knows she would hate to be called that. She may have hidden here in Texas, but she'd never stopped fighting.

He'd already written the piece. Really, it wrote itself. While he was lying on his bed in his dark room, he heard the sounds of O'Toole's drifting up to him. The sounds of the jukebox gently vibrated the floors. It reminded him of the first night he met her. Then, he heard her voice echoing in his head, and he couldn't resist picking up his laptop. He had only planned to write a few words. He needed to make some notes before he forgot anything.

Now, he was hesitating to hit send. He said the holy words 'off the record'. No one could prove it, but he knew it would ruin any ounce of trust she had in him. Mac stared at the blinker as it flashed on the screen of his laptop. He slid his hands off the keyboard and reached over to grab the paper. Her heart-shaped face looked back at him in gray newsprint.

There was something about Bailey Reynolds. He'd seen that sort of sadness in a thousand other eyes. They'd been victims of war, political asylum, and natural disasters. They were all taken from their homes, haunted by life, or simply living with less than they needed to thrive. That look drove him home, across the globe, and back to New York. Why was she different? Why did he think he could help her? Why did he *need* to help her?

It was her smile that hooked him. It was both wry and humble. That was a combination he couldn't resist. He didn't know if she was going to apologize and try to run away again, or pull her shoulders back, lift her chin, and tell him to take a hike. How could he convince her they were okay right where they were?

"Safety," he muttered to himself as the pointer hovered over the send button. "That's what she needs." He spent years trying to help others find safety in war-torn countries, but how was he going to help a scared single mom find herself a safe place in his arms?

He shook his head and slowly closed his laptop. It wouldn't be like this. He couldn't hit send. He flipped the paper over so he couldn't see her face before picking up his phone.

"Hey, Nana, do you have some time?"

His grandma's soft voice was barely audible through the phone. "Mac. Oh, my boy. It's good to hear your voice. I was getting worried."

"I'm sorry. Work has me traveling, and things have sort of gotten away from me. How are you?"

"Fine, except that darn cook keeps making the biscuits rock hard. Doesn't he know who he's feeding? I swear there's probably only twelve people with actual teeth in this place."

Mac stifled a laugh. "That sounds terrible! The canasta is still good, though?"

"Well, Betty hasn't left her room all week, and I caught George cheating last week!"

"Nana, that place is falling apart!"

"Boy, don't snap at your grandma. Growing up with your father...your mother, bless her soul, would never have tolerated half of it."

"Yes, Nana." He could practically feel her eyes roll. "Actually, that's why I called."

"Oh, really?"

"Yes. Well, I met someone."

"A woman?"

"Yes, but Nana, you know that's not always expected anymore."

"Save that for later. Tell me about her."

"Well, she's from New York, but she's living in Texas with her little girl now."

"A mom, huh?"

"Nana, I didn't call for an interrogation."

"What did you call for?"

"What does a woman need to feel safe?" Mac coughed to clear his throat. "I thought I knew, but I realized I've never really known a soft woman."

"I don't know one soft woman," Nana scoffed, "Just being a woman is tough."

Mac nodded, even though he knew his grandma couldn't see him. "Yes, you're right, but she's different. She grew up with fancy plates and private schools. She lived in the same house her whole life. I bet she went to prom, and the first car she learned to drive was a BMW." He paused. "Nana, what do I know about any of that?"

"Boy, you know plenty." Nana sighed. "Sheesh, if nothing else, you knew enough to call me."

"Maybe. I'm thinking I don't know anything anymore."

When Mac hung up the phone, he had a small smile on his face. He still wasn't sure what he was doing, but he was forming a plan.

Chapter Thirteen

Bailey

"Seriously?" Bailey held the phone closer to her ear.

"Well, I mean, yes..." the voice on the other end of the line answered.

She looked out the kitchen window and watched while Jackson carried a long two-by-four into the barn. "How many reporters?"

"I counted three before I called," said the receptionist from Rosie's school.

"Sarah Ann, I'm so sorry. I didn't expect them to show up at her school!"

"Oh, hun, they should be the ones apologizing. You'd have thought their parents taught them better. The audacity to just show up here!"

"Yeah..." Bailey was already sliding her jacket on and grabbing the keys sitting near her purse. "I'm on my way."

"We'll have her here waiting for you."

The kitchen door slammed behind her, and Bailey felt her

anger rising. "How dare they?" Slamming wasn't enough. She wanted to stomp and scream and holler. "Jackson! I'm headed into town. I have to go get Rosie. Don't you dare do anything dumb while I'm away."

"Is everything okay?" he yelled back from the barn.

Bailey barely heard him over the truck's engine rumbling. "It's going to be." Rocks flew and her tires slipped as she dropped into second gear, then shifted into third as she tore down the driveway.

What would her mom do? Those reporters wouldn't have jobs if Sherry Ann Reynolds was still here. The gall of those people. Predators, that's what they were, and her child was the prey. It couldn't keep going on this way. It would not go on this way.

Her teeth squeaked as they ground against each other. "Don't let them get to you. That's publicity rule number one. Don't forget that."

Hadn't she expected this? Maybe. Maybe not. Her home in Texas had always been a haven. They'd never tried to find her here. She'd occasionally have a call. Sometimes they'd request a quote, but she'd never had journalists stalking her on her doorstep.

As she pulled into the paved roundabout at the school, she swore and growled out, "Are you kidding me?"

She was expecting the press. What she hadn't expected to find was Mac standing on the front steps of her daughter's school, and he was the only reporter in sight. She asked herself, "Maybe Sarah Ann was wrong?" For an infinitesimal moment, she could feel the anger slipping away before she pulled it back around her like a cape. *"He's one of them, Bailey."*

"You talking to yourself?" asked Mac as she stepped down from her truck.

"Where did they go? Why are you here?"

"If you knew there were reporters here, why are you surprised to find me?"

"Well," Bailey paused, and said, "Sometimes I forget you're one of them."

Mac squinted into the Texas sun, which was beating down on them. He watched as she shrugged and knocked the strap of her sundress off her shoulder. Who knew how dangerous a $10 piece of fabric could be? "I asked them to leave."

"Nicely?"

"Well, no, but if my boss asks, tell him yes."

"Who were they?"

"Riffraff. I'd like to say it's going to get better, but it won't."

"What happened?"

"Have you checked your phone today?"

"Clinton called, but I don't want to talk to him."

"Bailey, it's a good thing you have that man on retainer because I don't know how he tolerates you." Mac took a step down the school stairs. "Your ex and your father announced their case against you today. It was in the papers...and it doesn't really make you look good."

"They're going to play the victims here?"

"It doesn't help that no one has heard from you. The

'grieving heiress' excuse only lasts so long." Mac took another step towards her and looked her in the eyes. "Look, these guys, they're vermin. They wanted a story, and they don't care if it's trash. I made it hard for them, and they left, but this is only the first wave. This story is catching traction, and if you don't get ahead of it, you're going to end up under it."

"I have been on the loop end of my daddy's lasso my whole life, and I'm tired of being pulled around behind him."

"Then you're going to have to figure out how to get ahead of him."

"What if he runs me down, Mac?"

"He's going to have a few people to go through before he gets there."

Bailey looked over Mac's shoulder towards the rusty red and brown brick building holding the most precious thing in the world to her. "This could hurt Rosie."

"Not more than hiding away in a hole and waiting until the rats find you to nibble your toes."

"Mac, that's dark and, well, sort of gross."

"Yeah, but I mean it, Bailey."

He finished stepping down the low flight of stairs that led up to the front doors of Rosie's school. "Go get your kid, call your attorney, come to terms with what's about to happen. When you've done that, then call me. We're going to tell every-one your story."

Bailey felt heavy. She was used to the weight of the Texas sun and a blanket of humidity, but Mac was asking her to take on the mantle of a celebrity again. Would she be any better at it with age and experience added into the mix?

Chapter Fourteen

Bailey

"It's official. We are no longer friends."

Bailey said, "Come on, it's not that bad."

"You are asking me to pull together an entirely new wardrobe. Not just a hey, I need to cover my body in something that's not plaid or denim, but I'll be wearing it in front of every big name in New York and most of the literate Western World wardrobe. Um, yeah, that's a big deal."

"I'm sorry," Bailey said, "You're right, maybe it's unfair of me to ask." Bailey sighed, and said, "Clinton and Mac say I need to do this. As soon as I get to New York, I'll have dinners and interviews...it's okay. I can call one of my mom's people."

"Don't you dare! Girl..." Taylor scowled and then smiled. "Bailey, this is so big. I'm honored you came to me, but—"

"It's a lot, huh?" Bailey pulled her friend into a hug. "I know, but I'm so glad I have you next to me."

"I'm not going anywhere...I mean, I need to get busy shopping, but then I'm right back by your side!"

A Stitch in Time had been three doors down from Patty Cakes for almost as long as Bailey had been in Texas. While it was a far stretch from Los Angeles, Taylor had never told Bailey what brought her to their little Southern town. Whatever it was, it was enough to know that her heart recognized a fellow survivor. "I want your name on everything. I want people calling you at 4 a.m. to beg you for your paisley overalls."

"You hush! Paisley..." Taylor scoffed and winked. "But, from your lips to the Lord's ears!"

A flash in the shop corner caught Bailey's eye. There was a small glass case nestled in the corner. Inside was a black pillbox hat with dark rhinestones and lace. "Is that new?"

"It just came in last week. Rumor has it Marilyn Monroe wore it while she was grieving after her divorce from Joe DiMaggio. Nearly impossible to prove, but it felt classy with an air of mystery."

"It does..." Bailey walked over to the glass case and asked, "May I?"

When Taylor nodded, she reached for the small black felt hat. The lace draped across her wrist and the afternoon sun through the front window display cast rays of light on the small, sparkling crystal chips stitched into the hat. Carefully, she lowered it on top of her head. A small mirror on the table next to her framed her face, and she reached up to pull her hair back. Beneath the felt rim, the lace shadowed Bailey's eyes. "If they want a grieving heiress, that's exactly what we'll give them."

"So, we're working with black."

"My mom's got to be rolling in her grave."

"Sherry?" Taylor laughed. "No, she'd be cheering you on."

"Well, she put me into this mess," said Bailey.

Whatever was coming, she knew one thing. She was going to need new clothes.

Bailey handed Candice a twenty and grabbed a small cardboard box off the worn counter at Patty's Cakes. "Thanks for watching her while I talked to Taylor."

"Rosie's so easy. She helped me frost some cupcakes for the High School bake sale Friday." Candice rearranged the lemon tarts in the display case and asked, "Was Taylor able to help?"

"She's going to try…I don't know what I'd do without you two. Your help with Rosie and both of you being here to see us through."

"Hun, that's what friends are for!"

"I wish you would let me help you."

"With what?" Candice waved a hand to gesture around the bakery. "With this? I'm going to figure something out. My mama always did, and I will, too."

"Your mama is a tough one." Bailey paused before she said, "How's she doing?"

"The doctors say she's doing well. It's just that her mind isn't what it used to be. I still get to see her every Saturday at the home." Candice nodded to Rosie and smiled at Bailey. "Thanks for always being my family…I'm going to be okay…I promise."

"I swear, when I get through this, we're going to sit down and make a plan."

"I know we will. In the meantime, I have two questions."

"Go."

"One, where is that hot hunk of man that's been following you across the country? And two, why didn't you tell me you knew Dolly Parton?"

"Where did you—"

"There are pictures all over the paper! They're all from before...you know." Candice reached under the counter to grab a newspaper. She laid it open on the counter. Bailey's face was all over the front page. "You looked so fancy!"

"Dripping in diamonds and surrounded by celebrities? You know I never wanted that."

"Bailey, I know, but everyone looking at those photos is jealous of you. They want to know everything...the good, the bad, and the crazy."

"It's crazy! Candy, not being able to sneeze without everyone in the greater United States wondering if you're catching a cold. That's not normal, and it's not how I want to raise my daughter."

Candice nodded and said, "It makes sense, but I don't think that's what your mom wanted for you."

"She wanted me to take over the family business."

"Yeah, but you don't have to do it like your dad did. All he wanted was the power it gave him." Dropping her finger on the paper, "I mean, look at Dolly. She lives big, but she also helps others. You could, too."

"You aren't wrong."

"Compromises will need to be made...like talking to the press."

Bailey shot Candice a look and then glanced over at Rosie.

"Are you thinking I should talk to any journalist, or do you have one in mind?"

"Girl, you know exactly who I'm talking about." Candice avoided making eye contact with Bailey. "He came into the shop earlier. He's a good tipper."

"It takes more than that to earn trust, Candy."

"I know, but it goes a long way in my book."

"Hm." Bailey pulled out and sat down on the small cafe stool tucked under the counter. "I think I'm ready to talk to him."

"I'm glad. You need to tell someone what happened."

"Yeah, I needed to talk to Clinton first."

"What did he say?"

"The probate process is progressing. My father's new attorney contacted him. Hugh hasn't officially filed anything, but Clinton is trying to move forward as fast as he can to force his hand or get to a point of no return that will defuse any claim my father might try to make on Ladder H Distilling."

"From what the paper is saying, your dad isn't happy. He's been to nearly every high-level event in the last week playing the grieving widower and telling everyone how you're taking away his legacy."

"Mac said the same thing. I just don't know how anything I can say could change where this is going."

"Well, I'd say Clinton and Mac are probably more qualified to tell you that. If they say you need to talk to the press...Bailey, hun, you need to talk to the press."

"Does 'but I don't want to' count?"

"You tell me..."

"Ugh, fine."

"Call Mac, like right now. I'll keep watching Rosie and you can go talk to him."

Bailey's palms felt sweaty as she dug out her phone from her back pocket. His number was still on the now-dirty white card she had tucked away in her purse. Every ring felt like a lifetime. She was almost ready to hang up when his deep voice said, "Hello?"

"Um, hi."

"Who is this?"

"Yeah, I'm sorry. I know you weren't expecting a call."

"Bailey?"

"Can we, maybe, if you're not too busy, meet tonight?"

"Tonight?"

"Well, you know, if you can."

Mac's voice was so deep she could feel it vibrate through the phone. "Bailey, for you, my night's wide open."

"Oh...okay."

His laughter rolled across the line. "You sound surprised."

"No...just, well, I don't know, Mac."

"You think going on an official date with me is a bad idea?"

Bailey gripped the phone and shot a panicked look at Candice, then squeaked, "Date?"

"Well, isn't that what you're asking?"

"No!" Bailey yelled into the phone. "I mean, I could see why you'd think that, but no. Definitely, no."

"Yeah."

"I wanted to talk about the story for your paper."

"Yeah."

"An exclusive! I talked to Clinton today. I was thinking about what you said."

"Yeah."

"You're sounding like a broken record. I'm sorry, Mac, I should have started there."

"No, it's fine. It's okay. Yes, I'll tell your story. I'm glad you trust me enough to help you with that." His voice was soft in her ear. "I want you to trust me, Bailey."

She swallowed the knot in her throat. "Maybe someday, Mac."

"Just not tonight." Mac coughed, and his voice took a professional tone. "Ms. Reynolds, I'd love to hear your story. Where can I meet you so we can discuss the article?"

"Mac, really?"

"I propose the steak place off Main St."

"A Rare Affair?"

"Sounds fitting. 7 p.m.? Meet you there?"

"It's a date. I mean, yes..."

"Bailey," he growled. "See you then."

She hung up the phone and looked at Candice before saying, "Tonight. 7 p.m."

"Girl, I don't know what's wrong with you."

"Neither do I."

Chapter Fifteen

Bailey

She walked up to the large wooden doors of A Rare Affair. The restaurant featured modern food culture with a Texan-sized love for red meat. New York trends with a Texas spin. Patting down the hem of her skirt, she reached towards the black wrought iron door pull. It didn't matter what she told Mac; this felt like a date.

While getting ready, she thought about wearing jeans and a sweater—the baggier, the better! But when she started thinking about the way he felt pressed up against her in that small dark NY bar...she kind of wanted to feel that way again.

There was a swirling fear in her gut. Not the same sour mix of anxiety and bitterness she'd had thinking about being in the same room as her father. No. It was a low ache, a nervous flip, a tickle of butterfly wings. Did Mac do this to her? Or was it the shifting changes in her life and the promise of a fresh start if she could just push through the next few months?

She'd shaved her legs. That was for Mac. Her thoughts were a mix of next steps and what to do, mired in feelings sprinkled with thoughts of brown eyes, a deep voice, and the tickle of a trimmed beard as it slid across her neck. "Pull yourself together, Bailey," she growled.

"Are you falling apart?" His voice washed over her from behind.

The hair on her neck stood up, and she felt instantly na ked...vulnerable. In her distraction, she walked right past him. Pivoting on the heels of her practical pumps, she turned to meet his eyes. "Mac, I didn't see you there." The dim lighting of the restaurant allowed him to hide in the shadows. Ferns and Ficus filled the corner, leaving him guarded and shadowed like a predator on the hunt. Was that comforting or scary as hell? She trusted him to keep her safe, but she didn't trust herself to be alone with him.

"I'm sorry," he said, and his lips cracked into a crooked smile. "I didn't catch you off guard, did I?"

"Not at all," said Bailey, as she gripped her purse tighter and smiled back.

Before Mac could comment on the obvious lie, the server was grabbing menus and guiding them towards their table. "I hope you don't mind, but I asked for a table in the back. I thought some privacy would be best."

"That sounds nice." Bailey was relaxing in the restaurant's quiet ambiance. Dark woods, soft leathers, and dynamic metal fittings gave the restaurant a swanky men's club vibe. The only thing missing was an impermeable cloud of cigar smoke and the stomping slap of penny loafers. It reminded her of the better parts of her childhood.

"What are you thinking?" Mac asked as they settled into

their seats. He slid a glass of water closer to her.

Bailey whispered, "I'm wondering if this is what hope feels like?"

Mac paused and then took a drink of his own water. His eyes watched her over the glass. Their warm brown depths were full of questions, too. "What are you hoping for, Bailey?"

"It would be so easy to say freedom, but it's much more complicated than that."

"Safety, family, stability." He looked her in the eyes. "Maybe, love?"

"Those are things every human wants, Mac."

"True."

"So, even you?"

"More so lately. For a long time, I didn't think those were things I could hope for, either." Mac watched her across the table, his eyes growing deep in the dim lighting of the restaurant.

"I'm in a fight for my mother's company, my daughter's life is changing, and my past is coming back to haunt me. Do I have the option of hoping for those things?"

"It sounds to me like financial freedom, a world of new beginnings, and a life you never thought was possible for you and your daughter. You can have a life lived on your terms."

"You make a living telling stories, Mac. You make it sound way too easy...and way too tempting."

"Bailey, it's all right here. You just have to ask for it." He reached across the table to trace his finger down the back of her hand. "Ask me for everything. Tell me what you want the world to see."

She could feel the soft fabric of her dress slip across her

knees as she shifted in her seat. "I want them to respect me but leave me alone."

"That will all come with time. If I've learned one thing in my two decades as a journalist, it's that hype fades and interest wanes. In two weeks, it will be something else. Hell, it could even be two days. Not that you want to wish for a natural disaster or put ill will on another person, but, as my Nana always says, this too shall pass."

"I've used that on Rosie, myself." Bailey leaned back as the server delivered two glasses of red wine to their table.

Mac lifted his in a toast. "May you live as long as you like and have all you like while you live."

Bailey lifted her glass and clinked it against his. "To hearts filled with hope and dreams that grow bigger than wishes."

"Cheers." Mac took a sip and nodded as Bailey sipped hers and then puckered her lips. "That bad?"

"No, I'm sure it's a lovely vintage." She swirled the wine in her glass. "I grew up around all of this...sommeliers and imported wines. The bar was always stocked with the best liquor a person could buy." Her nose crinkled, and her lips pinched. "I just don't like it!"

Mac feigned shock. "The shame!"

Bailey laughed. "I'm good at faking it, though."

"Have a few more sips of that," he said, and pointed to her glass. "I'd like to talk to you about something, and I think it will make that easier."

"Uh, oh."

"I wrote something already."

"How?"

"After the fireworks."

"That's not the story I want them to know!"

"It's the truth."

"That they won't believe. It will sound like puffed-up accusations. It will look like I'm just throwing mud."

"Read it. Then decide. It's only a first draft."

Bailey twisted the cloth napkin in her lap. "What's the twist? What spin did you put on my story?"

Mac leaned back in his chair. "I told them everything you haven't. Not the messy stuff, but the secret parts of you that you've kept hidden...your life as a mom, how much Rosie loved her grandma, what you've done with your little Texas farm. You've built walls and kept your family safe, but to those who are on the outside, you feel very far away. A tower, not a gate. I want them to be curious. I want them to knock on the front door so you can let them in for tea."

"That's the respect part."

"Yes, in part, but it's also the human part. You aren't just a New York socialite. You're the girl next door."

"That doesn't sound awful..."

Mac shook his head. "Bailey, there is absolutely nothing awful about you."

Her breath caught, and she whispered, "Not a date, Mac."

Two hours later, Mac still made it feel like a date. He was funny, handsome, and she couldn't remember the last time she'd had such a good time. Well, that was a lie. She could. It was both the best and worst day of her life. Walking into O'Toole's Tavern after her mom's funeral felt like a last-ditch effort to unload her feelings at the end of an unspeakably long day, but it had also been their beginning. Bailey kept trying to get rid of him, but he just kept showing up again.

It could have been the wine or the warm Texas night air as they walked towards the Rare Affair parking lot, but she felt hot. Restless in her bones. Ready to dance, yell, toss up her arms, and just spin under the dark arch of stars. He was right next to her, and she knew she should get into her car, but...she couldn't walk away from him. She was in trouble, ready to do something reckless, and all it would take was a whisper...three words, I want you.

His hand reached out to steady her as she stumbled on the warm asphalt. "I think you're going to need a ride home."

"I could call—"

"Jackson? No."

"Candice. She has Rosie."

"Where is she?"

"The farm."

"Rosie will be in bed. I'll take you."

He watched her pull back her hair and laugh. That evening was a reminder of better days. He forgot how it felt to ache for someone. Even more, he'd forgotten how to just have fun. Sure, he could still hit the town and have a night with the guys, but it was something different to be surrounded by the smell of her warm skin and the twinkle in her eyes when she teased him.

She leaned towards him, and he could feel the warmth of her breath on his neck. His chin dropped, and he took a deep breath. Roses, sunshine...and the sweet smell of a woman. He reached out to put his hand on her hip.

"You okay?"

Bailey looked up into his eyes and nodded as she said, "Yes," and bit her bottom lip. "But I need to get home."

Mac traced his hand down the side of her face. "I'll take you." He wanted to respect her decision to keep this professional, but, more than that, he wanted to bury his face in her neck and pull her close. "If you don't kill me first."

Bailey glanced up, her brows furrowing in confusion. "Me?" she asked, her voice barely above a whisper. "Why would I do that? I know I was... unkind...when we first met, but I can't quite explain it..." She paused, her gaze drifting to the side as she gathered her thoughts. "I think I owe you an apology."

Mac stood by the car door, his hand resting gently on the frame to ensure she didn't hit her head as she leaned down to slide into the passenger seat. "You don't have to explain to me how you felt," he said, his voice soft yet firm. "Lots of journalists don't have great reputations."

Bailey nodded, her eyes reflecting a mix of understanding and regret. "Well, and I do have a history of avoiding the press, but..." She reached out, her fingers lightly brushing against his hand as he prepared to close the door. Her touch was tentative yet warm, conveying her sincerity. "You haven't shown me any reason to mistrust you. I judged you too harshly." She looked up at him, her eyes filled with newfound trust. "Thank you...for being someone I can trust."

Chapter Sixteen

Mac

His Nana told him Bailey needed to trust him. That he should make her feel safe and not push her. Mac knew he needed to show her what sort of man his grandma raised him to be. Bailey had finally given him her trust and said it out loud, but he wanted to be more than her favorite New York journalist.

The urge to hold her close was distracting as hell. Having her near him was a constant temptation. He wanted all of her. *Now.*

On the other hand, Bailey wanted to take things as slow as molasses. He knew her past, and her present were colliding, and rolling around in the hay with him was the last thing on her mind. His grandma had also said she would need time, and that old woman was almost always right.

Mac looked over at Bailey. She'd fallen asleep with her head resting against the window. He couldn't imagine how tired she must be after years of fighting for herself and Rosie, or how much work months of caring for her dying mother had been.

He knew the last few weeks of probate proceedings, funeral affairs, and dealing with her father had left her hollowed out with fatigue. Bailey needed to rest. He should have taken her home sooner, but he'd enjoyed the last, sweet hours laughing with her. He felt a tug of disappointment as he pulled up to the driveway that led to the Ladder H Ranch.

Hung from stout poles, there was a thick wooden sign carved with the Double Hs that made up the Ladder H logo. He turned right and drove slowly down the long gravel road to avoid waking her up. She snored softly in the quiet car. It was inevitable. This evening was coming to an end, but he wanted to drag out every second.

He rounded the last curve in the driveway, a small bend of trees before the fence surrounding the farmhouse opened to a large, round driveway. "Dammit!"

Bailey startled awake, "Mac? Is everything okay?"

He looked out at a cluster of cars and three white vans with antennas and satellite dishes mounted on top. They were parked in front of the house with their headlights pointed in various directions. Lights lit up the front of the house and the spot where Candice stood on the porch with her arms crossed. People were walking around between the cars when a camera crew started racing towards them.

"Who are they?" she asked, her voice still thick from sleep.

"I'll take care of this. You get behind your friend and get into the house."

"But, Mac—"

"I'm going to go around them to the left. It will put you near the foot of the stairs." He gunned the engine and kicked up gravel as he cut off the camera crew from the pack of journalists.

"I'm going to need a new driveway after all this." Bailey ran her hands down her face, grabbed her purse off the floor, and said "Well, you sure know how to show a girl a good time."

Mac laughed. Even under siege, she had it all together. "Don't come out until they're gone. Don't open the door for anyone. I'll call you when it's safe."

Bailey nodded, then bobbed forward as the car jolted to a stop. Candice was already down the stairs, helping to open the car door.

"Bailey! They showed up about fifteen minutes ago. I called the Sheriff, but you beat her here."

The woman ran up the stairs hand in hand as Mac threw open the driver's side door and jumped out to confront the camera crew, hoping to intercept Bailey as she ran into the house.

Rosie pushed open the front door, and Candice and Bailey banged through, "Mom!"

"Rosie, close the door!" Bailey could hear the reporters yelling in the drive.

"Ms. Reynolds!"

"Just a few questions!"

"Are you taking the company from your father?"

Bailey looked at Rosie's pale face and Candice's worried eyes.

"I tried to call you," said Candice.

Rosie nodded, "We were worried, Mom."

From the bottom of her purse, Bailey pulled out her cell phone. "Dead. I'm so sorry, I didn't know."

Candice sank down into the old high-back chair next to the stone fireplace that covered half a wall in the living room. "I think we're going to need a plan."

"I don't think we're in Kansas anymore."

"Mom, that's silly. This is Texas."

Bailey pulled Rosie close and squeezed her tight. Over the top of her little girl's soft curls, she nodded to Candice. "We can't keep going like this."

Bailey packed another pair of jeans into the hard-sided suitcase on her bed. She needed a few things to tide them over while they got settled, but Taylor would send her fancy clothes soon.

They would stay at her mother's brownstone in Manhattan. The old brick building was located near Central Park, and Bailey kept reminding herself that Rosie would love the house and the nearby park. For all the years they'd lived in Texas, Bailey had never taken Rosie to see her grandma. Sherry had always been perfectly happy to come and visit her granddaughter on the old farm, and Bailey never asked to return to the metal and concrete jungle she had once called home.

This visit would be about more than offering respect for her deceased mother. Bailey didn't know how long they would be there.

First thing that morning, she'd asked Clinton to look into good elementary schools and then made sure that Jackson and Candice could watch the farm. Poor Captain Rainbow Furry Sparkle Pants was going to be missing Rosie's kisses and treats after school every day. Bailey worried about what would come next, but she knew her little girl was tough. Last night was just another reminder of how things had changed for her and her daughter.

While the sheriff's car had shown up with lights spinning red and blue soon after Bailey's driveway escape, it had still felt like hours before Mac called, and then softly knocked on the front door. The white vans in her drive had all disappeared. When she opened the door for him, he'd look tired...and worried. Before she could say, "I'm sorry" or "thank you", he was already talking.

"Were you able to get Rosie down? Are you okay? Did you get hurt getting into the house?"

He'd all but patted her down and tucked her in before he'd been on his way.

She couldn't do that again. More so, she wouldn't. New York had security details, bellhops, and private entrances. Her privilege protected her there, and Clinton could run guard against her father's attacks. She would no longer be prey.

A door slammed outside, and she peeked out her bedroom window. "Rosie, Candice is here! Is your bag ready?"

"Almost!"

The floorboards squeaked under her feet as she went down the old, narrow hallway. Photos of her, her mother, and Rosie as a baby lined the house's old beige walls. Generations of her family had made a home here, and she hated leaving. It felt like she was running away. "It's just for a little while," she whispered and ran her hand along the roughly textured wall.

Rosie was standing on top of her suitcase, jumping up and

down. "It won't close!"

"Let's take a peek." Bailey opened it and watched as a stuffed bunny, three pairs of pants, and six dolls fell out onto the floor. "I thought we were only packing what we needed."

"I need my dolls, Mom."

"Girl, I need my chaps and my purple Ariats, but I'm not bringing them." Bailey leaned down towards Rosie and pulled her close for a hug. "Hun, we'll be back before you know it."

"Mama, what if we won't?"

Giving her daughter an extra squeeze, she said, "Rosie, I want to make you so many promises, but I can't. I don't know what the next few months will bring. I don't know if we'll come back to the farm soon or if we'll need to stay in New York. But I promise we'll be back here. Even if it's only for holidays, visits, and to load a moving van to the brim with your dolls."

Rosie picked up her favorite Barbie, a brunette dressed in a cowgirl outfit. "I'll bring Sage and maybe one more..."

"Bailey? Are you here?"

"Jackson?" Bailey hollered back at him and then pointed to her daughter's dolls on the floor. "Rosie, how about you bring two dolls and a few extra outfits for them?" A car horn honked in the driveway. "Can you be fast? We don't want to miss our flight."

She thumped down the stairs to find Jackson waiting by the front door. "I wanted to make sure you had everything you needed before you left town."

"What would I do without you?"

Jackson laughed. "I thought dating a doctor was hard." He pulled her close for a hug. "Jet setting off to the Big Apple and leaving me here to take care of Captain Sparkle Pants."

"It's a good thing you're so good at taking care of all the ladies in your life."

He winked and smiled. "It's a tough job, but someone has to do it."

With her suitcase in hand, Rosie pulled on the edge of his shirt. "Don't forget, Mr. Jackson, to give Captain grain. He likes that best, and don't let him eat the trash." She held up her hand to cover her mouth. "Mama doesn't like that!"

He patted the top of her head and winked. "You got it, Ms. Rosie. No garbage and lots of grain."

Bailey pulled Jackson in for another hug. "Thank you...we'll be back home soon."

Chapter Seventeen

Bailey

New York was loud. Even though Bailey was used to Captain Sparkle Pants bleating from sunup to sundown and Jackson's nail gun echoing through the barnyard, this was different. She'd forgotten how grating the sirens and constant murmuring sounds of people living their lives were. Manhattan was a step above basic New York living, and the upper floors of her mom's townhouse were quieter, but she missed the midnight hours of owl song and silence.

They'd been in New York for a week. Rosie loved the small ice cream shop down the street. Her favorite afternoon activity was to grab a single scoop waffle cone and walk around Central Park while looking at the various dogs and city goers fleeing the chaotic energy of the busy streets.

Clinton said the probate process was going well, though her father was still contesting her right to inherit the Ladder H. Jackson said the farm was doing well, but that Candice was bringing the goat pastries, "because he looked sad." That morning, Rosie asked to take a video call with the animals and spent an hour making goat noises in the second-floor library.

Each day felt crammed with things to do, but also purposeless. Bailey was box checking and trying to learn how to run a business she'd only ever observed from the sidelines. Earlier in the week, Bailey took a tour of their downtown office and sat through a two-hour-long meeting with the board. Her dad might not have been pleased about her taking over, but the board members seemed thrilled. Clinton couldn't answer all her questions, so she hired an accountant on retainer to evaluate the company's current market strategy and investment portfolio. She couldn't help Ladder H if she didn't even understand how it ran. Her head was floating with profit and cost matrices, and she'd finally understood the joke about TPS reports.

It was Wednesday. She needed to get Rosie back into school. It had only taken a few days in the city to know that waiting to enroll her daughter would be a bad idea. Her little girl was just as bored and restless as she was.

"Mom! The mail is here!" Rosie yelled, as a pile of envelopes slid through the mail slot in the front door and cascaded to the floor. "Can I help today?"

Daily, the tidal wave of correspondence came into the brownstone. Requests from media outlets, condolences from friends and family, and way too many catalogs littered her desk. Who knew Sherry liked online shopping so much? "Sure, hun, let's take it to the living room."

It was still weird to sit on the embroidered velvet couch without her mother offering her a cup of tea. The plastic crinkled as she sat down, but it felt too soon to change anything in her mother's...her...home. "This looks like a card. Would you like to open it?" Bailey asked and gave a pink envelope to Rosie.

Carefully sliding her mother's rose gold letter opener along the envelope flap, Rosie tore the paper open and pulled out a creme card covered in wildflowers. "Sending our cond...oh...lens...es for your loss."

"Condolences."

"What does that mean?"

"It means they're sorry grandma died."

Rosie nodded, "I'm sorry, too."

"Me, too, bug." Bailey picked up a crisp white envelope and slit it open. "An invitation. I was wondering when those would start arriving." As she read the card inside, her back stiffened and her eyebrows drew together.

"Mom?"

"Hm?"

"Are you okay?"

Bailey stopped reading the card and looked at her daughter. "Yeah, I'm sorry. I just need a minute."

"Did a sad card make you cry?" Rosie walked over to her mom and wiped a tear from her cheek.

"It's kind of sad." Bailey pulled her daughter close for a hug and tucked the card underneath her. "Can you go play in your room?"

When she could hear Bailey's feet stomping on the floor above her, she grabbed her phone and waited for the line to stop ringing. "Hello?"

It had been a week since she'd heard Mac's voice. Maybe she was making a mistake. "Hi, I'm sorry."

"Bailey?"

"Yes, it's me."

"Is everything okay?" She could hear Mac moving something around on the other end of the line. "You're in New York, right?"

"Yes. That's why I'm calling."

"Oh?" Did she hear a whisper of hopefulness in his voice? "I didn't want to bother you while you were getting settled."

Bailey pulled the envelope out from underneath her. Her hand clasped the paper's rough edge. "That's very kind of you...um..."

"Yes?"

"Well, something happened."

"Is Rosie okay?"

Bailey closed her eyes and took a deep breath. "My father sent me an invitation. He wants me to join him at a dinner party he's hosting in honor of my mother. He thinks it would be good for everyone to see us as a united front. I guess she was planning it before she...passed away...and he didn't want to cancel it."

There was silence on the line.

"Mac?"

"Yeah, I'm sorry. I know you didn't call me as a journalist." He sighed. "I'm trying to figure out the right way to reply."

"I don't need words, Mac. I need you to help with Rosie." Bailey paused and listened to see if she could hear her daughter's little feet close by. "She doesn't know anyone else in New York."

"Does that mean you're thinking about going? Is that—"

"Mac, don't ask me if it's a good idea." Bailey stared up at the living room ceiling. Off-white plaster medallions surrounded the polished brass fixture.

"Well, you know it's not. Have you called Clinton?"

"It's for my mom, not my dad."

"You know that everything your dad does is ultimately for him."

"Yes, but—"

"But, Bailey? Really?"

"It's fine, you don't—"

"Stop. Yes, I do. I just want to make sure that you know what you're getting into first." Mac's voice was muffled when he replied, "Where are you, and when do you need me?"

"Thank you, Mac." Would she regret playing into her dad's hand? She heard Rosie singing upstairs and wondered if any of this was ever going to get any easier.

Chapter Eighteen

Mac

Mac stood at the base of the townhouse steps, exhaling slowly as he took in the whitewashed brick and arched entryway that framed Bailey's new life in Manhattan. The elegant structure loomed before him—a stark contrast to the sprawling Texas ranch she'd called home for years. It was strange to think of her here, where the pace was relentless, the air thick with city noise, and anonymity was as much a commodity as wealth.

She hadn't belonged in Texas, not entirely, and yet no one could say she truly belonged here either. At least, not anymore.

Pressing the heavy wrought-iron knocker against the door, he let it fall once, twice—then a third time before his hand dropped to his side. From inside, he heard the sudden burst of movement—light, excited footfalls pounding toward the entrance. His lips turned slightly at the edges, already knowing exactly who was about to greet him.

"He's here!" Rosie's high-pitched excitement rang through the entryway an instant before the door flew open, revealing her beaming face.

Mac's amusement was short-lived as Bailey's voice sharply followed from inside the house.

"Rosie Ann Moore! I told you not to open the door!"

Rosie, completely unbothered, turned to look back over her shoulder. "But he's not a stranger, Mom!"

Mac watched as Bailey rounded the corner into view, her posture tense, her movements sharp—but when her gaze landed on him, something in her eyes softened. She wasn't irritated that he was here. She was irritated because she wasn't used to needing to worry about things like locked doors.

"I didn't say he was, you didn't check, and you aren't a grownup," Bailey countered, placing a gentle but firm hand on her daughter's shoulder. "Please go clean up your dinner plate in the kitchen while I show Mac around."

Rosie exaggerated a dramatic sigh, rolling her eyes straight at him like they had an inside joke Bailey hadn't been clued into, then turned and disappeared down the hall.

Bailey lingered in the threshold, hesitating for only a beat before stepping aside to let him in.

"I'm sorry..." she muttered, folding her arms instinctively across her torso as he brushed past her into the house. "It's just—she's not used to New York. No one ever came to the farm that we didn't know, and—"

"You don't have to explain it to me, Bailey," Mac interrupted before she could finish convincing herself that he needed an excuse. "I want her to stay safe too."

Bailey exhaled, her relief more visible than she probably realized. If he had to guess, she'd been going nonstop since she arrived in the city. He didn't doubt she was doing everything in her power to keep Rosie from feeling the strain of the move, thrusting herself into maintenance mode, tackling each issue methodically. But that took a toll.

"You wouldn't believe how relentless they are here," she continued, her tone lowering as if the walls had ears. "Mac, I swear they never stop coming."

"You knew that would happen," he said, watching her closely. "This is exactly what we talked about before you left Texas."

"I know," she admitted, her hand coming up to rub her temple. "I just hoped...well, I wanted them to back off when your story came out."

Mac's stomach tensed. He wasn't proud of how that had played out. He'd protected most of the things she'd wanted to keep private, but the press didn't care about nuances. No matter how careful he was, no matter how much restraint he exercised, people were going to find ways to twist her narrative into something more scandalous.

"Yes, we gave them some of what they wanted, but—"

"But a grieving heiress and a decade-old scandal begets more."

Mac didn't need to be told that. He knew the moment the article ran that it wasn't going to be the end of it. If anything, it stoked the flames. Everyone was watching now, fascinated by the power struggle, the drama of her inheritance, her estranged father, her return to high society—hell, even her love life. Jesus Christ.

"The paper is already asking for another exclusive," he admitted. "But I told them they need to be patient. That nothing has fundamentally changed. This was always a part of our strategy, remember?"

Bailey's eyes flickered with something unreadable. "I hate that story."

Mac already knew which one she meant.

"'Ms. Reynolds, forced to flee her home for the safety of her daughter, fears retribution from her father while resolving her mother's estate.'" She recited the words with disgust, her fingers tightening at her sides. "You won't tell them about tonight?"

His expression hardened.

"Not everything is about you, me, and the paper," he told her, his voice dropping lower. His gaze lingered, drinking in her form—careful, deliberate. The black silk dress hugged her frame with breathtaking precision, the material shimmering under the dim light of the foyer. "Some things I want to just be about you and me."

Her breath caught.

His chest tightened.

Bailey stood before him in that high-necked, devastatingly elegant gown, her blonde hair twisted into an intricate sweep that left the graceful curve of her neck exposed. His fingers itched to run along it—to explore where her pulse fluttered, to feel the warmth of her skin under his touch.

"Us?" Her voice was the softest whisper.

His attention lingered on the way the glittering rhinestones at her feet caught the light, then traveled back up to the bare plane of her collarbone.

"Us," he confirmed, the word slipping from him like an

oath.

She took in a sharp breath, her lips parting slightly, but whatever she'd been about to say was lost when he reached for her.

His palm skimmed the curve of her waist, drawing her to him, and the moment she was close enough, he lowered his mouth to hers. Their lips met in a slow, deliberate kiss—no hesitation, no ambiguity. His hands settled at her hips, pulling her firmly against him. She was warm, soft...and for the first time since he'd met her, she wasn't resisting him.

Mac tilted her chin higher, deepening the kiss with quiet insistence, savoring the way her lips molded to his and the way her breath hitched as his fingers teased against the silk at her back.

This was exactly how their first night should have ended. Not with unanswered texts, or with a missing moment, but with her surrendering to his touch.

A sharp voice shattered the moment.

He gently positioned her a step back and let his hands slip away from her, though his gut screamed in protest. Rosie's voice carried from the kitchen. "Mom! Can I have some ice cream?"

Bailey lifted her palm instinctively to her throat, the color high in her cheeks.

"That's how I wanted that night to end." Mac exhaled through his nose, still tasting her on his lips, glancing quickly toward the hallway as Rosie came into view.

"Mom!?" Rosie repeated, blinking up at her mother expectantly.

Bailey was still flushed, still gathering herself. "Yeah...yes..

.yes, you can have some ice cream," she answered, shaking her head slightly like she was pulling herself from a fog.

Mac ran a hand through his hair, still feeling the slow, smoldering burn of where her body had been pressed against his. Even after she pulled away, his skin still tingled with the phantom traces of her warmth, the scent of her perfume lingering in the air between them like an unspoken invitation.

She reached for her purse, and his gaze followed the elegant curve of her arm, the way her fingers brushed against the polished surface of the foyer table. Her breath was slightly uneven—barely noticeable, but he caught it. Caught the way she swallowed, the tiniest hesitation in the movement, as though she was as reluctant to step away from him as he was to let her go.

"You better get out of here," he said, his voice huskier than he intended.

She wobbled slightly on her heels, regaining her balance with a soft intake of breath. The sharp contrast of her in this space, in her sleek black dress and delicately pinned hair, against the memory of her barefoot in that seedy bar—laughing, spinning, untamed—had been throwing him off since the moment she'd opened the door to him tonight.

"Mac, there's enough ice cream for you, too."

He had to smile at that—at the way she said it, like it was an afterthought, but her eyes gave her away. She didn't want to leave him yet.

"I'm craving...something else," he murmured, his gaze flicking to her lips. There was no mistaking the way her cheeks deepened in color, the way she stilled as if waiting for him to do something reckless. He wasn't sure if she would have let him, but he didn't want to push her too far.

Instead, he let it sit between them, watching the way her mouth parted slightly before she turned away, stepping toward the door before she could change her mind. The city air rushed in as she descended the steps, the echoes of car horns and distant conversations swallowing her whole. He could still taste her on his lips, could still feel the hint of her body pressed against his chest—too brief, too fleeting.

She waved once before hailing a cab, but he saw the shift before she even stepped to the curb. Her expression shifted, the fire in her eyes dampening as her thoughts carried her somewhere else, somewhere heavier. Her fingers tightened around the strap of her purse like she was grounding herself, and he recognized that moment, that feeling, because he'd lived it too many times to count.

As the distant glow of headlights washed over her, illuminating the set of her shoulders, the tilt of her chin, he felt a pang of something akin to protectiveness curl low in his stomach.

Something had changed.

He watched her climb into the cab, and though it carried her away into the night, the weight of whatever haunted her lingered in the air between them.

What would Hugh try to do to her tonight?

Would she want to come home and tell him?

Did she know it was about more than the story for him?

Chapter Nineteen

Bailey

The cab pulled up in front of her parents' building—wait for the door, slow pivot, smile. It was part habit and part instinct, but one hundred percent familiar. This was what New York felt like to her.

Clicking heels on asphalt and an attentive doorman. The fluid motion from car to door to elevator. She walked, pushed forward by the building's staff. They all knew her, and she barely knew them. A constant rotation of people who catered to her needs.

As a child, she tried to befriend them. She tried to show them her pretty shoes and the rocks she found on the streets, but her father had always frowned. "We don't associate with the staff."

Sherry had always given a wry smile and a modest nod, but Bailey only heard her talk to the staff when her father was gone. There were tidbits of gossip, and they all knew to maintain the facade. As she stepped onto the elevator, she wanted to ask,

"Where was Gerard?" or "Does Maria still hide candy in her pockets?" But this wasn't Texas, and she had a role to play.

Bailey shifted on her heels as the elevator began the ascent to her parent's penthouse suite. The dress Taylor sent her felt like armor. The sleek, black silk gown hugged her athletic frame. Calvin Klein would never approve of her curves, but hours in the saddle had shaped strong quads and round glutes. She could tell Mac enjoyed watching them as she walked out.

The gown featured a high neckline with delicate lace detailing that added a touch of sophistication. Her shoulders were bare, showcasing the divots in her collarbones and enhancing the curve of her breasts. The black silk flowed seamlessly down to the floor, with a subtle train that swept behind her as she moved. Taylor's design was part grieving heiress and part evil queen. To top it off, she'd added the black pillbox hat above a tight french twist. Bailey wore the hat at a slight angle that allowed her to hide her eyes behind the hat's light tuft of tulle and black rhinestones.

When the elevator opened at the top floor, she pushed back her shoulders and took a deep breath. A butler stood at her parent's door, and she could hear a harp playing. "Welcome, Ms. Reynolds," he said, as he opened the door and let the music roll out into the hallway. "It's good to have you back."

She paused before stepping through the doorway, and her shell cracked. "Hi Gerard, I missed you."

He gave her a half-bow. "If you need anything."

"Thank you," she gave him a wink. "I know where to find you."

Entering her parents' home was like traveling back in time.

There were the same high-back chairs flanking the hallway to the sitting room and the same floral wallpaper her mother purchased in France when she was ten, but slight changes caught her eye. There had always been a wildly enormous bouquet on the front hall table, which now sat bare. Her mother would have been at the door to greet her, and now a young woman was leading her back to the living room. The house was just as lovely, but the warmth was all gone.

"I was wondering if you'd come."

Bailey barely avoided the jump scare. "Ethan, I was wondering if you'd be here."

"Thinking of me, then?"

"Not at all." Bailey lifted an eyebrow and said, "Only thinking ahead to avoid you."

"There was a time—"

"Which is long gone." She stepped back as he stepped towards her.

"Imagine, Bailey, we could have everything we'd always wanted. Rosie would have a family, the Ladder H would keep growing, and your dad...he would accept it...eventually. We'd have an empire."

"An empire? Really, Ethan. It's a fancy distillery. It's the same moonshine my uncles were making in their backyard stills three decades ago. Throw in some uppity booze, and we're just catering to the elite masses. You aren't saving the world with liquor."

Her ex scowled, and his lip twisted. "The Ladder H legacy is mine. Rosie is mine. You were never good enough."

"That's where you're wrong." Bailey straightened her knees

and stood as tall as her three-inch heels would let her. She poked her finger into his chest to emphasize her words. "Rosie has a family, and I was always enough. You didn't deserve us." She was ready to pivot on her red-soled pumps and walk right back out the door with a message for Gerard to pass along to her father...*bite me.*

"Ethan, you found her." Hugh's rough voice was all she needed to put her armor back up.

Bailey turned to meet her father's eyes. "This was important to Mama."

Her father nodded. "It was, it most definitely was." He placed his hand on her back and moved her to the dining room. "Please, join us. We're just about to take our seats for dinner. You've arrived just in time."

She shifted her shoulders to move his hand off her back, but he continued to drive her forward. "I know where I'm going."

"Of course," he looked at her and smiled. "How silly of me."

Hugh was never silly, charming, or flattering. What the hell was going on? Bailey paused as the wait-staff pulled out the chairs, and she tucked her dress underneath her as she sank down into the old mahogany chairs lining the long dinner table decked out in crisp linens with sparkling crystal and bone china. He sat at the head of the table. Ethan was to his left and Bailey to his right. She looked across the table at Ethan and glared. "Get your foot away from me."

"Now, children," Hugh said, with a small smile. "Let's keep things amicable in front of your mother's friends. Remember," he said and looked at her before finishing. "We're here for her." At that moment, his mask dropped. The jovial host was a dried-up curmudgeon. She's seen that same impatience and frustration in his eyes before. An 'issue with the staff' or a 'disappointing employee' always preceded it. Bailey spent most of her childhood avoiding him or hoping that she was never the reason that look crossed his face.

Yes, Papa almost fell out of her mouth before she pinched it back.

Once all the guests had settled in their seats, her father slid back his chair and stood up. The edge of his knife clinked on his half-filled wineglass, and the tinkle of crystal shifted all their eyes to him. The vacuous faces of the New York elite watched her dad. Had her mother really been friends with these people? She knew they weren't all what they portrayed on the outside...any more than she was, but it was such a long shot from the Sherry she knew. Her Sherry would sit making cupcakes for hours with Patty for the school bake sale or put a chain back on Rosie's bike when a reckless jump had knocked it off.

The Sherry these people knew was a member of the country club. She was pristine, and there was never grease on her hands. Bailey didn't know how to make both things fit, but her mom had done it. She'd walked the line.

"Thank you all for coming today. It may be in poor taste, but I know that my dearly departed Sherry would have wanted us to gather as friends for a cause near to her heart..." Hugh's voice droned on. Yes, her mother would have wanted them all together. Yes, raising money for the schools in Harlem was a good cause. Yes, Bailey wanted to offer whatever support her mother needed—even in death, but Hugh was a blowhard and listening to him blather on was torture.

"Even in a time of hardship for our family, it's important we unite for the greater good of our community. I only wish our dear granddaughter, Rosie, could have joined today. It would have warmed Sherry's heart to see those she loved the most come together in a difficult time, rather than pulling apart. She never liked watching people she loved fight. She always loved that our business focused on our family and the families of our employees."

Hugh looked down at Bailey and then over to Ethan. "Our family gave so much to the success of Ladder H distilling, and Sherry spent the better part of her life taking care of those she loved. I know, even in her last moments of rest, that she wanted us joined together, not tossed asunder." He raised his hands to place one on Bailey's shoulder and one on Ethan's. "We're here to show you today that our family is stronger than ever and there are no plans to change Ladder H management." He squeezed her shoulder and then dropped his hands to his side.

As he sat back down, light applause filled the room, and he smiled at Bailey. Lead settled in her blood, and her face felt like it was burning up. How dare he? She hated her daughter's name in his mouth. He wasn't the patriarch of the family. Her chair was scraping across the hardwood floors before her brain caught up to her legs. Anxiety smacked her in the gut when she glanced down the table at the faces of New York's most influential families. Hugh adjusted his dinner coat and leaned back in his chair. His smile would have rivaled the Cheshire Cat.

Run. That's what she wanted to do, but that's not why she'd come home to her New York roots. She could feel the

Texas earth pumping through her blood. It was calling her home, but she wasn't unfamiliar with her father's game. It was about money, promises, and popularity. She'd never liked to play it, but she was here as the grieving heiress. If she backed down now, he would win.

"It was generous of my father to respect my mother's dying wishes this evening. Sherry has been supporting and contributing to the Harlem Foundation for as long as we've lived in New York. She was never one to support injustice." Bailey looked at her father and spoke to him instead of the rest of the room. "Gosh, and she just hated bullies. She always said, every child deserves a voice and a safe place to grow up."

The room sat silent, but she could see a mix of confusion and respect on the faces surrounding the table. "I also respect her last wishes and will fight to manifest them." Bailey held out her hand and looked at the server nearest her. "My purse, please."

Wait staff shuffled to move her chair and pivot out of the way as she walked through them. Bowls of soup rattled on trays, and a tea server was nearly upended in the hall.

Glancing back over her shoulder into the room, she said, "If you'll excuse me, it's time for me to get started on that."

Murmurs and whispers followed her to the entrance, but she didn't care anymore. None of this was about her. She kept hoping her dad would change, but she needed to grow up and accept that he never would. Hugh wanted his business more than he wanted a family, and, for Sherry, that business had been her family. It was time for Bailey to treat it the same way.

Gerard startled as she threw open the unit's front door.

"Madam!"

She pulled him into a tight hug and then let him go. "Thank you...for always watching over us."

"It was my pleasure," he said, before readjusting his jacket and reaching for the elevator button. "Your mother wouldn't have had it any other way."

Bailey smiled. "No, I don't think she would have."

Chapter Twenty

Mac

He stared at his phone, the dim glow of the screen illuminating the tension tightening his jaw. No call. No text. He exhaled slowly, rubbing at the back of his neck before setting the device down beside him on the nightstand. His fingers drummed absently against the wood as he wrestled with the pull in his chest—the restless anticipation that had been gnawing at him since Bailey left her father's dinner party.

What happened last night? Whatever it was, it ignited something in her. She threw herself into the moment, brimming with something close to exhilaration—a fire in her eyes he hadn't seen before. Watching her pace the townhouse, her words tumbling over each other as she recounted the night's events, had only deepened the intrigue she already held over him. He couldn't get enough of it—of her. She had been sharpening herself against her father's cruelty for years, but last night, for the first time, she wielded that sharpness with purpose.

She was coming alive in this fight.

Still, no matter how composed she may have been, he knew that being back in New York wasn't easy for her. There were shadows lingering just beneath the surface, ghosts of a past she'd fled but now had to face head-on. He wanted to know how she was holding up. Was she still riding that rush from last night, or had the weight of it all settled on her shoulders now that the spotlight wasn't shining so brightly?

He wanted to be there, to see for himself. Or, at the very least, to hear her voice.

But she hadn't called.

When he left her home, he promised to see her soon. But when he asked her to call him today, she hadn't been in the same room with him. Wherever her head had been, it was buried in a time long gone. Distracted wasn't the right word...determined. Bailey seemed hell-bent to shake free of her father, and he knew it wasn't the right time to distract her with them. But he'd have traded all the land in Texas last night for one more chance to taste her lips.

When his phone suddenly vibrated against the woodgrain of the nightstand, he snatched it up so quickly that he nearly fumbled it. But when he saw the name flashing on the screen, disappointment curled in his gut.

Not Bailey.

Still, the call wasn't unexpected. He let out a measured breath and pressed the phone to his ear.

"Hello?"

"I'm surprised you answered."

Mac pinched the bridge of his nose at the sound of James' familiar voice. "James."

There was a pause, then the chair creaking on the other end of the line told him exactly what was coming next—James settling in, bracing himself for a conversation he already knew wasn't going to go in his favor.

"Yeah, man, I'm sorry. I've been trying to keep the line open. I'm expecting a call. You don't need to worry, though. I've got a good lead."

"I've worked with you for years. Don't start that with me. Where's my story?"

Mac leaned back against the headboard, running a hand through his already disheveled hair. "Well—"

"No."

There was another pause, followed by a sigh that carried the weight of exhaustion and frustration.

"The Post published a story this morning. Ladder H Heiress Goes Toe-To-Toe Defending Her Right to the Throne. Why didn't we get this? I thought you had an in with the girl."

Mac's jaw tightened as he swung his legs over the side of the bed. The words on the page might have been different, but the approach was all too familiar—sensationalized, exaggerated. They made it sound like Bailey had been trading blows in a boxing ring instead of standing her ground at a dinner party laced with veiled threats.

"They're making it sound like it was a heavyweight match with Vegas odds. James, it was a family dispute over dinner."

"In front of half of New York."

He fought the ripple of irritation rising in his chest. "Sure, there were some big names there, but it wasn't—"

"Mac, you don't make those calls."

Mac's fingers flexed over the phone. "You've never doubted my judgment before."

"I've never had to! Clearly, this girl's got something that's messing up your head."

He exhaled sharply through his nose. "My head is fine. In fact, it might be straight for the first time in ages."

If James caught the shift in his tone, he didn't acknowledge it. Instead, he coughed and spoke with deliberate patience, as if explaining something to an obstinate child.

"I don't want to hear that, Mac. If these are the calls you're making, maybe you shouldn't be making them. You've got me worried."

Mac's fists clenched against his knees. He didn't want to lose this job. Not because of James' threats. Not because of pride. But if he lost this assignment, he would lose his leverage. If someone else took over the story, it wouldn't be just another ambitious journalist—it would be someone who wouldn't hesitate to dig deeper, to push boundaries Bailey wasn't prepared to have crossed. And, when the press stopped treating her like a headline and started treating her like their next fat paycheck?

They would tear her apart.

His stomach turned at the thought.

He had to stay in control. For her.

James wasn't done. "She just mentioned it in passing?"

Mac swallowed and reached for the old beer sign hanging in his window, running a finger absently along the chipped paint.

"Your job is to chase leads!"

He let the silence stretch. He wasn't about to hand Bailey over to the press the way James expected him to.

"There isn't a news story here, James," Mac said finally, his voice steady. "These are people trying to work through the aftermath of a death in the family while the world watches. We're feeding the vultures, not writing breaking news."

"That is the news, Mac," James countered, his voice loud, raw with frustration. "Hear me when I say this won't happen again. All eyes are on this story, and it's driving sales. We absolutely cannot—no, we will not—miss another break in this story. If you can't handle that, I'll find someone who will."

Mac's grip tightened around the phone. "Fine. I hear you."

He knew James' warning wasn't an empty threat.

He wouldn't let that happen.

"I'll work harder to make sure you get the story first."

James exhaled, content with the answer. "That's what I like to hear. I'll consider that a promise."

Mac remained silent as his editor hung up.

The second the call ended, he checked his phone again. Still no messages. No missed calls.

His lips pressed into a thin line. "There won't be a story if she's not talking to me anymore."

Navigating his way to their most recent conversation, he hovered over the keypad. His fingers paused over the buttons, considering the right words. Something neutral, something that wouldn't push—something that might get him an answer.

Instead, he locked the phone and let it slide onto the nightstand.

His grandmother's voice curled at the back of his mind.

"She'll come to you when she's ready, Mac. If she doesn't, then she was never yours to begin with."

Mac exhaled through his nose, staring up at the dark ceiling.

He hated waiting.

But for her?

He would.

Chapter Twenty-One

Bailey

The plum-colored velvet fell off her shoulders in loose folds. Taylor had an eye for fashion that flattered, but she'd outdone herself. Where the black silk dress she'd worn to her dad's dinner party felt like preparing for war, this dress felt like slipping on sensuality.

Soft fabric and loose lines wrapped around her hips and draped down her thighs. Bailey had forgotten what it felt like to feel unstoppable while embodying sensuality. Dating hadn't really been at the top of her list after she left Ethan. She could have blamed it on a thousand things. The first of which would have been Rosie, and trying to keep it together as a single mom, but, in truth, she hadn't wanted to open her heart up again. She filled it, instead, with her daughter and their small ranch in Texas. Was there any sense in making room for more if it was going to hurt her in the end?

Dinner party invites had been rolling in, along with happy hours and cocktail lunches. For a girl raised around liquor, it was clear she was grossly out of practice drinking it. Tonight, her head felt light and bubbly, like the champagne they'd been pouring all night at Manhatta.

Clinton said that going out was important. She needed to rekindle old friendships and let people see her as she truly was. Every big name that supported her was one less person who would help her father. Allies and enemies...it was all coming back to her.

How to drop a subtle comment but deny it three minutes later. The giggling confusion mixed with a tilted chin and whispered gossip. To these folks, it was a game, but to her, it was a means to an end. Bailey wanted her mom's estate resolved and her daughter to be safe. Clinton wasn't wrong, but she missed the moist air and soft night sounds of her country home.

The cab ride home gave her time to sit with her loneliness. The numbing power of champagne and laughter softened Bailey's worries and doubts, but left behind a gnawing ache to see her best friend.

Bailey climbed the steps up to the townhouse, paid the babysitter the nanny agency sent, and then climbed the stairs to her bedroom, where she took off her shoes and kicked them into a corner. The slinky dress that made her feel like a goddess all night fell off her body to land as a shimmering pile of fabric on the floor. As she slipped out of the elastic and plastic contraption that had been holding her boobs hostage all night, she sighed. The cotton nightgown she pulled on felt like butter on her skin.

Before she thought to check what time it was, her fingers were already dialing the call. Just as her head hit her pillow,

Candice's voice filled her ear. "Are you safe? Do I need to help you hide a body?"

"Not yet, but I can't make any promises for the future."

"Okay, we'll hold that option in reserve."

Bailey wiped a tear from the corner of her eye. "I'm so lucky. This is all just awful, but I am so grateful I have you."

"Ditto."

"Did I wake you up?"

"No." Candice grunted a bit. "I'm caught in a tailspin. White Claw and Netflix have me deep in their grip."

"Aw, hun."

"I'm glad you called. It's been weird with you gone."

"Come here." The words poured out. "Come to New York!"

"What about the bakery? The farm?"

"Meh, Jackson said he had another month until his next big job. He can cover the farm for a few more days. Do you have any big orders coming up?"

"No, not really." Candice sighed. "Just the regulars stopping by the shop each day."

"How about I place a big order?" Bailey sat up in her bed. "It's about time I hosted...something."

"Are you suggesting I go to New York and bake for your fancy friends?"

"Yes." Bailey grabbed a pen and paper from the small nightstand next to her bed. "Anything...whatever you want. We'll have a team of caterers to do your bidding, and Rosie can make her debut in the New York circles."

"But—"

"I know! We can throw her a birthday party!"

"But her birthday was two months ago."

"Right, but she's never had a big birthday party. Not like this, and no one here knows the actual date. It will be symbolic. Like a new start."

"Well, it's not a terrible idea, but—"

"But nothing, no is such an awful answer. Anything you need...money to cover time away from the bakery, your airline tickets." Bailey paused and whispered into the quiet on the line. "Please..."

"It could be good for marketing..."

"Say yes!"

"Yes!" Candice laughed.

As plans solidified, like the faint outline of a dream taking shape, she realized something else—she was accepting this life. She wasn't just stepping into a role out of necessity; she was claiming it. Claiming her mother's legacy. Claiming her place back in New York. And, more than that, ushering Rosie—her bright, innocent little girl—into a space that had once made her feel like she was drowning. With careful actions, she could make it better for her daughter. She could open doors rather than close them.

Though they planned Rosie's birthday ball as a modest affair, Bailey knew it would be unforgettable. This party wasn't about the press, or her father's influence, or ensuring the world saw what she wanted them to see. It wasn't about strategy or positioning for control. It was for Rosie. A moment tailored entirely for her daughter, free of any obligations beyond joy.

It was close to one in the morning when Bailey hung up with Candice. The old clock on the mantle clicked forward another minute, carrying with it an unnerving silence. Her gaze drifted around the room, settling on the papers scattered across her mother's desk. Threading through the disarray were the remains of her old life, the delicate gold embossing of an invitation from one of her mother's oldest friends, an envelope containing a thinly veiled legal threat from her father, and an abandoned clipping from The Post detailing what they deemed her declaration of war at dinner.

Her fingers hovered over the headline.

It made it seem as though she'd stormed into the dining hall with legal briefs and a sword. In reality, she had simply held her ground, choosing not to cower beneath her father's presence. If people thought that was a battle, then perhaps they had no idea what she was truly capable of.

But even as the memory of that night surged through her, electrifying her nerves with bitter tension, another thought pushed its way to the forefront.

Mac.

She had tried to keep her distance. Since the night he watched Rosie, she'd told herself she needed space. That it was necessary. Logical. That, of course, she should put a boundary between herself and the one person who could potentially break through the delicate walls she'd spent so many years constructing.

A journalist. A journalist who had been hired to tell her story. Who had every reason to maintain distance, to be objective, to simply watch her life unfold rather than entangle himself in it.

Only, he had entangled himself. And she let him.

Because, despite how impossible it was and how irrational it would be to let herself trust him—she missed him.

She missed the way his voice dipped into something rougher, quieter, when he spoke to her. She missed the way his hands felt, the way they didn't just touch, but they held. Like she wasn't an obligation or a complication. Like she was his.

Her hand tightened around the phone.

A siren wailed from the nearest block, tapering off into distant city noise. A taxi door slammed shut somewhere on the street, layered with slurred goodbyes in thick Brooklyn accents.

Would he be awake?

She glanced down at her phone, the blue-white light from the screen illuminating the delicate ridges of her knuckles. 1:11 a.m.

"Make a wish," she murmured absently, as though the quiet superstition would grant clarity.

Her thumb hovered over his contact.

The damn journalist should be the last person she called.

She touched his name anyway.

It rang only once.

"Hello?" His voice was thick with sleep, slow and warm. "Is everything all right?"

The sound of it sent a pulse of something deep and hot through her stomach.

"Mac," she breathed. "Hi."

She shouldn't have called. But hearing him—just from that one word—was enough to wipe away any hesitation she'd had leading up to this moment.

"Bailey?" The way his voice shifted was subtle, but she recognized it. Sleep was pulling away, and now there was something else, something aware. "I'm sorry—" He cleared his throat, his voice dropping an octave. "I wasn't expecting..." He hesitated. "Are you okay?"

His concern curled around her, softening the weight in her shoulders.

"I'm sorry to call so late."

"You know you can call anytime."

Anytime. She shouldn't have been comforted by that, but she was. Instead of answering, she let the silence stretch, not knowing what to say without revealing too much.

He picked up on it immediately. "Bailey?" A pause. "Why the late call? I can't think of a good reason for New York's trending socialite to be calling me in the dead of night. What is it?" His voice softened. "Do you need a babysitter?"

She swallowed, suddenly nervous, but forced herself to push through it.

"No. Despite Rosie's complaints, I've hired someone else."

"Ah," he murmured thoughtfully. "That makes sense."

There was a shift.

She felt it.

The unspoken question hanging thick between them.

His voice, slower now, coaxing.

"I haven't heard from you."

She hesitated, fingers tightening around the edge of the

desk. The truth was complicated. The silence hadn't been intentional—but maybe part of her had wanted to see if she could pull away. If she could let him slip into the background like so many others had.

It hadn't worked.

Because here she was.

Her throat tightened.

After a long pause, she exhaled.

"Can you...would you, maybe, come over here?"

Silence.

His breath hitched on the other line, barely audible, but noticeable enough that she felt it.

"To your place?"

The hesitancy she expected wasn't there. Something twisted in her stomach.

"Where's Rosie?"

"She's sleeping," Bailey murmured, barely able to get the words out fast enough. "I just..." She exhaled slowly, pressing her forehead into her palm. "I don't feel like being alone right now."

The word hung between them...alone.

She stopped herself from biting her lip. Coward.

Bailey took another breath before adding, "Well...and I have a story for you."

A moment of quiet.

Then, his voice dropped, the heat in it unmistakable.

"Bailey, do you really think you need to bait me with a goddamn story?"

No.

She didn't.

She closed her eyes, tilting her face toward the ceiling as she absorbed the sound of him.

"I just meant—"

"You meant you miss me," he murmured.

Her breath caught.

There it was—laid out, raw and undeniable.

Mac wasn't the type to speak in riddles. He didn't make things difficult for the sake of dragging a reaction out of her. He was direct, every move deliberate, and she liked that about him.

"...not everything I do is about getting your job done," she said after a moment.

"I know that," Mac replied, his tone gentler.

Bailey hesitated.

"I don't want to make things harder for you," she admitted, voice quieter now. "Things at The Globe must be a mess right now."

"My job is not your concern."

"But—"

She stopped as he cut her off, his voice calm but firm. "Bailey."

Silence stretched between them.

Then...softer. "Can we talk here?" Her voice was barely above a whisper. "It's just...so much easier when you're close."

Another pause.

This time, she heard him inhale sharply through his nose.

The answer came swift, absolute. "I'm on my way."

Chapter Twenty-Two

Bailey

Gray sweatpants looked ridiculously good on him.

Bailey had barely opened the door when Mac stepped inside. Tousled hair, sleep-creased clothes—God, he looked like he had just thrown himself together and caught a cab straight over. Maybe he had. She wanted to invite him to go back to bed—since he had clearly just left his own. Instead, she stepped back, just enough to let him in, but not enough to break the tension between their bodies.

Mac's gaze flickered down, like he was assessing her, reading the shift in her posture. Then, with deliberate slowness, he lifted his hand towards her.

"Come here."

Bailey stilled, chest rising once before she let out a breath and closed the space between them. She made the first move. She'd asked him here. And yet, here he was, grounding her. Reeling her in like he belonged to this moment just as much as she did.

Her fingers found his palm, sliding against the warmth of his skin, and his grip fastened around her hand.

Yes. This. Exactly this.

She lifted her chin slightly, the barest hint of a challenge creeping into her smile as she pressed the flat of her other palm lightly against his chest. His heart beat steadily under her fingers, solid and strong. He hadn't shaved today. It was ridiculously appealing, the scratch of scruff lining his jaw, and she pressed her lips together to fight the urge to tilt her head back and explore the sharp angles of his face with her mouth.

She missed looking at him. She missed touching him.

And dammit, she wanted to be touched back.

"I'm not afraid of you," she said, her voice softer than she intended.

Mac's head tipped slightly, something unreadable flickering across his face.

"You aren't?" he murmured, his voice low and rough. His thumb traced lightly against the inside of her wrist, his breath warm as he looked down at her. "That's good. I don't want to scare you." His grip on her hand tightened, just slightly, just enough to keep her in place. "But...maybe...you scare me a little."

Her lips curled, teasing. "Oh?" She rose to her toes, just enough to reach him, pressing a soft, lingering kiss at the corner of his mouth. His hand flexed against her waist. Encouraging, but not possessive.

"But why?" she asked, drawing back just enough to glance up at him beneath dark lashes.

He was so warm. Heat radiated from his body, effortless and intoxicating. She wrapped her arms around the breadth of his shoulders, shifting against him until she could mold herself completely into his chest.

Mac exhaled slowly, his hands settling at the small of her back in a way that made her nerves hum. His voice was thick with something unspoken when he admitted, "No one else has ever made me feel...so aware. And I'm worried I'll do this wrong."

Bailey stilled, surprised at the hesitation she heard from him.

She tilted her chin up, meeting his gaze. Something in that admission—the raw honesty of it—made her stomach flip in an entirely new way. She was making him unsure? The thought sent a thrill through her chest.

She smirked slightly, loving the contrast of knowing she made him want and knowing she was the one who could put him at ease.

"Wrong?" she echoed playfully.

His Adam's apple bobbed slightly before his voice dropped even lower, eyes never leaving hers. "Scare you away...or make you feel unsafe."

Bailey's mouth parted slightly, startled by how much that admittance affected her. She pulled him closer, sealing any remaining space between their bodies.

"Mac, you don't make me feel unsafe." She ran her hands slowly down his back, enjoying the play of muscle there. "Not anymore."

He tensed. Just slightly. Then—stepped back.

"See." He ran a hand through his hair, nearly laughing in exasperation. "I never wanted that."

She heard the unspoken "It kills me that I did."

"You were a journalist," she reminded him. "And I have a very complicated history with journalists. I didn't know who you were that night in the bar, but I knew what you were."

"That's fair," he admitted, laughing again, this time at himself. He pulled her back in with the ease of someone who knew she wasn't truly trying to escape. His lips brushed her temple—so light it almost didn't touch at all.

"Let's agree," he murmured against her hair, his voice full of promise. "What we do is separate from who we are...always."

Bailey nodded slowly, nuzzling against him in silent agreement. Then, she ducked her head back to peer up at him.

"Yes," she said, "but sometimes...they can overlap."

Her voice was coy, light. It was half an answer, half a tease.

He lifted a brow at that, latching onto the implication immediately.

"Is that why you called me here?" he asked, his fingers teasing at her lower back. "To overlap?"

Bailey hummed lightly, shaking her head against his chest. "Nope," she whispered, her voice filled with a teasing sort of warmth. "This was definitely why I called you."

Mac inhaled sharply, pulling her against him. He tilted his head down, his lips grazing her cheek, drifting lower toward her jaw.

Her stomach tightened in anticipation.

"Good," he murmured, brushing her skin lightly as he spoke. "Because I'd hate to disappoint."

His breath against her skin sent an ache through her chest.

"Now that you bring it up, though..." She inhaled deliberately, forcing herself to step back, knowing full well what she was doing. She caught his gaze, her lashes flicking upward again, full of playfulness and promise. She pulled him by the hand toward the study.

Bailey wanted more. She wanted this—wanted to tease him, drive him a little crazy. Drag him upstairs, press him against the mattress, and feel the weight of him press into her in return.

But she also wanted him to ask. She wanted to feel the moment when his restraint snapped, when all the careful holding back melted into finally.

They needed this little game.

She needed it. Needed to stretch the tension between them so tight that when they finally unraveled, she could feel the unraveling everywhere.

Mac followed, undeniably aware of her intent.

He looked at the chaotic stacks of paper throughout the room.

"Did your office explode?" he asked dryly. "Where did all this paper come from?"

She smirked. "Hush." Bailey settled onto the desk in front of him, crossing one leg over the other. "Clinton keeps sending me papers, I keep getting invited places, and there are so many things I need to sign. I think they multiply while I'm sleeping."

"I know a guy," Mac said, his voice dipping lower. "He's a private investigator. I've used him for other stories."

Bailey lifted a brow, pulling her fingers away, feeling the phantom heat where their skin had barely touched.

"A PI? For your Globe story?"

"I guess," Mac confirmed, studying her, something unreadable flickering across his features. "But that's not you, or us, or this...I want to do this right. I think he can help."

She exhaled, leaning forward slowly, deliberately closing the gap between them. His eyes shifted, flickering down to her lips for a second too long. She had him now.

A slow smile curved across her mouth before she murmured, "I think I can use all the help I can get."

"If the amount of paper littering this room is any indicator, you're probably right." He pointed to a stack of papers. "I see you saw The Post article."

Bailey's expression flattened slightly.

"Yes," she said, reaching for the newspaper. She folded it in half before tossing it toward the already overflowing waste bin. "And we could have done that better."

His lips twitched. "My boss thought so, too."

Bailey rolled her eyes. "Doesn't matter. That's old news."

Mac studied her, then leaned in slightly.

"Oh, really?" His voice dipped lower.

"Work or pleasure?"

"Hmm," he growled. "I am definitely not thinking about work now, but I think you are, and if we get that out of the way, I can convince you to think about pleasure."

Her fingers were toying with the hem of her nightdress as she lifted a brow. One step forward, and her mouth was inches from his. One shift of her hip and her lips brushed his with aching, teasing slowness, no hesitation, no second-guessing. His sharp intake of breath was exactly the sound she wanted—needed—to hear.

"That's some quality thinking." She nodded, settling her

gaze on him with quiet intent. "I want this out of the way before we..."

"Yeah?" His hands closed around her waist, anchoring her flush against him, the heat of his body pinning her into the edge of the desk as his lips claimed hers in return. He grumbled, "These tempting little dresses you wear."

Bailey lifted her hand to trace a finger down the edge of his jaw, along the length of his neck, to settle in the hollow V at the base of his throat. "I said I missed you...I want you. I want us. And the only way that's going to work is if you get the scoop on our next story."

His slow smirk curled dangerously.

"Ours?" he echoed, voice laced with possibility.

Bailey bit her lip and nodded again, pulling him closer.

"Yes," she whispered. "Ours."

"So, now that the work is out of the way." Bailey leaned back against the edge of the wooden desk, letting her fingers trail over the papers scattered atop it. She'd been keeping Mac at arm's length for days, but now, as he stood before her, his presence filling the small study, she was acutely aware of the pleasure he was promising her. "What do you think?"

She missed this—the slow burn of his presence, the way his unwavering gaze always seemed to see right through her, the raw pull in her stomach when he took a step closer.

His voice, low and edged with curiosity, cut through the tension thickening the air between them.

"Rosie's party could earn you a lot of empathy."

"Yeah, but it's about taking back the dialogue from my dad, too."

She caught the flicker of something in his expression—comprehension, yes, but something deeper buried beneath it.

"Well, absolutely. But it's also letting people look behind the wall you've built to protect your family."

His voice sent a shiver down her spine, and she stiffened slightly, hating that he always had a way of cutting straight to the heart of things. He wasn't wrong. That was exactly what unsettled her the most.

Bailey turned to face him fully, tilting her head slightly as she studied him. Her hands drifted back, propping herself against the desk as she crossed one leg over the other, letting the hem of her silk robe slip just a little higher on her thigh. Not intentionally—not entirely—but the way his gaze flickered downward for the barest second sent heat curling in her stomach.

She wanted to see that look in his eyes again, the one that told her he was fighting himself, fighting whatever this electric charge between them was. Because she wasn't going to resist him. *Not tonight.*

"Bailey, why are you fighting this so hard?"

She exhaled, slow and deliberate, before answering. Not about him. He meant the story.

Right. The story.

"You don't know what it's like to be on the opposite side of the camera, fighting to tell your side of a story. It's harder when the stories are about you."

"I've seen people who would compromise every one of their morals to have the popularity and social clout you possess."

She let out a soft, breathy laugh, tilting her chin up to meet his gaze. He was close now. Not close enough.

"But I never wanted it, Mac."

Her voice was quieter now. She didn't need to say it loudly; he was right there. Close enough that she could have lifted her hand a little, pressed her fingers against the unshaven line of his jaw, traced the rough edge all the way to his lips.

Instead, her fingers curled back around the letter, the rough texture grounding her.

His eyes scanned her face like he was memorizing the way she looked in the low light of the study, and for a moment, she forgot the conversation. Forgot everything except how dangerous it felt being this close to him again.

Her voice came softer now. "These were my mom's last words to me."

He reached towards the letter before she could stop him. His fingers were brushing deliberately against hers. She sucked in a slow breath, keeping her composure in place through sheer force of will.

"What did she say?"

Bailey didn't answer—not immediately. Her fingers skimmed along the folds of the paper as she pulled it open, shifting enough so that his chest nearly grazed her shoulder. Almost. Not quite. It was a balance she wanted to tip, to see exactly how much more he could take of this.

That's when the key tumbled from the folds of the letter,

clattering against the rest of the paperwork.

"Oh."

Mac lifted a brow. "What's that for?"

She swallowed, reaching for it. "I forgot about it." She held the cool brass between her fingers, running her thumb along its worn edge. "Does it look familiar to you?"

He reached for it slowly, his fingers closing over hers in the transfer.

Not a brush, not an accident. *Deliberate.*

Every nerve in her body was tensing. His touch was warm, grounding, the rough pad of his thumb teasing over hers in a way that sent an aching pulse straight through her stomach.

"It looks commercial."

"I thought the same thing. Maybe a post office box or a safe deposit box? The teeth didn't match any of the other ones on the old key chain Clinton gave me."

Mac studied the key, but his gaze lifted before she could pull her hand back. "Do you trust me?"

She sucked in a sharp breath at that, her stomach flipping at the quiet intensity in his tone. He wasn't just asking about the key. He was asking something else entirely.

"You keep asking me that."

His lips twitched, but there was no humor in his eyes. "It's hard to tell with you, Bailey."

Her throat tightened, pulse thudding in the quiet. He was standing too close, heat radiating from his body. She wasn't sure she'd ever wanted someone the way she wanted him now. That was the entire problem, wasn't it?

She'd run from this for a reason.

But right now...Bailey hesitated—for an instant—but her lips parted, her pulse visibly quickening in the delicate hollow of her throat. Mac caught the way her fingers tightened slightly where they rested on the desk, how her stance shifted almost imperceptibly toward him.

Yeah. She wanted this as much as he did.

"Maybe..." she murmured.

That was all the invitation he needed.

Chapter Twenty-Three

Mac

"How about a tour?" Mac asked, his voice dipping lower. He reached out, tracing the backs of his fingers lightly along the length of her bare arm—a whisper of touch, enough to send a slow shiver through her.

Bailey blinked, slightly thrown off balance. "A tour?"

"Mm." His smirk deepened. "It might be in a townhouse, but I'm still just an Ohio boy who knows nothing about all this fancy Manhattan living. It'd be a shame not to have the full experience."

Bailey rolled her eyes, but the curve of her lips betrayed her amusement. "You're ridiculous."

He grinned, letting his fingers skim down to lace through hers, giving her hand a gentle tug. "And yet, you're taking my hand anyway."

She sighed in mock frustration, but let him lead her out of the study, up the grand staircase, and toward the quiet warmth of the upper floors. He let her control the flow, taking his time, asking easy questions, nodding at little stories she shared about the house, the memories tucked into every detail. He wanted to see her relax, wanted to coax her out of the weight of the evening and into something lighter, something just for her.

When they reached the master bedroom, she hesitated in the doorway, glancing back at him. "Mac, I—"

He slid his hands lightly along her waist, leaning in enough so that his breath teased the shell of her ear. "You can tell me to stop," he murmured. "You can tell me if this isn't what you want." His fingers flexed gently where they rested. "But if you do want it...just say the word, Bailey."

Bailey's throat bobbed as she swallowed. Then, slowly, she turned in his arms, tilting her face up to meet his gaze. Vulnerable. Deciding. Mac stayed perfectly still, waiting.

Then—finally—she curled her fingers into the front of his shirt and whispered, "I want this."

Something inside him snapped.

Mac claimed her mouth with a low, heady groan, his hand threading into the soft waves of her hair as he walked her back into the room. Bailey gasped into his kiss, her hands running up his chest, her fingers twisting into his shirt as his lips coaxed her into opening for him. Slow. Deep. Not a kiss, but a claiming. A murmured promise against the heat of her skin.

Bailey shivered when he broke away, his mouth moving to the delicate column of her neck. Her breath came in soft, uneven pants as he traced slow kisses along her jaw, down to the tempting dip above her collarbone. She smelled like warmth—something sweet and impossibly soft—and it was undoing him one second at a time.

"Mac..." Her voice was a plea, her fingers flexing against his chest. He pulled back just enough to search her face, to read everything she wasn't saying out loud.

She wanted this.

She needed this.

And so did he.

It was still dark when he woke. The faint hush of early morning filled the room, and Bailey's soft snuffles in the dark made him smile. For a long moment, he lay still, watching the gentle rise and fall of her breathing, remembering the night before—the way she'd rested her head over his heartbeat, her laughter quiet and a little shy, the way she'd finally exhaled and let herself just *be.*

He remembered pressing a kiss to her forehead before she drifted off, her fingers tracing lazy patterns on his chest until sleep claimed her. She'd felt so small and sure at once, warm against him in a way that made everything else fade into the background.

Now, in the stillness before dawn, those memories settled around him like a blanket. He brushed a hand across her hair, careful not to wake her, and smiled to himself. *Well, hell,* he thought. *That's a sight I could get used to.*

He eased carefully out of bed, his foot finding the floor one inch at a time. Her breath hitched for a second, then evened out again. Mac sidestepped a pile of clothes, lightly kicked a shoe out of his path, and paused at the door. When he glanced back, she was still curled beneath the blanket, peaceful and beautiful in the half-light.

He closed the door softly behind him, the latch clicking shut in the quiet.

The hallway was quiet, and a long oriental rug absorbed the sound of his feet on the floor. Old photos on the hallway walls caught his attention. Golden frames held aged pictures of an old moonshine still and two young men standing next to it. There was a grainy photo of a young girl on a horse, smiling under her cowboy hat, and a wedding photo of a young couple in front of a small white country church.

Mac traced a finger along the edge of a frame. Smiling back at him was a young girl in a dress with a mountain of ruffles from her hips to her heels.

"That's Mom," a voice said in the dim light.

It took all his field training to slow down his heart and turn to the little girl with a smile on his face. "Hey, kid, it's late. What are you doing out of your bed?"

"I think it's early."

Mac glanced at his watch. The glowing numbers read 5:47 a.m. "You're right."

"Did you have a sleepover with Mommy?"

Mac took a step back and stuttered before he said. "Um, I wanted to surprise her with breakfast. I heard she really likes pancakes."

Rosie stood on her tiptoes and smiled. "She does!"

"Whispers! We don't want to wake her up."

"Oh, that would ruin the surprise." The little girl frowned and looked around. "A fire truck woke me up."

"Yeah?" asked Mac.

"Yeah, it's loud here." Rosie said, then turned and walked to the kitchen. "Let me show you where the things for the pancakes are."

"It sounds like you're having a little trouble getting used to things here."

"I miss Captain Rainbow Furry Sparkle Pants."

"Wouldn't that surprise people? Watching him walk down the street."

Rosie giggled and grabbed his hand to pull him down the stairs and around a bend into the kitchen. "He'd try to eat grandma's fancy roses!"

"You're right. I guess it's better he's back home on your farm."

The kitchen, lit by a small night light and the appliance's digital displays, cast dark shadows on Rosie's face as she looked up at Mac. "I wish I were with him," she whispered.

Dropping to his knees, he opened his arms. "May I give you a hug?"

She answered by wrapping her small arms around him. Rosie's body trembled in small sobs. Mac squeezed her and then let go. "Rosie, you are so brave. Just like your mom."

"Oh! She's the bravest! I never see her cry."

Mac winked at her. "Oh, she cries, but don't tell her I told you."

Rosie held out her small hand. "Pinky promise."

Mac entwined his large finger with hers. "Promise." He sat down on the tiled kitchen floor and tapped a spot next to him on the kitchen rug. "Can I tell you a story?"

"Yes!" Rosie squealed and settled down on the rug.

"Shh! We don't want to wake up your mom before the pancakes are ready."

"Oops." Rosie whispered.

Mac waved his arms dramatically and whispered, "A long time ago, in a place very far away..."

In a hushed voice, Rosie said, "That's how the good stories start!"

"There was a young boy."

"Was it you?"

"Questions at the end," Mac said with a smile. "The young boy traveled by bus, and by plane, and by boat to meet his father in a land unlike anything he'd ever seen before. There were tall buildings with roofs covered in gold and brass. The sunlight lit them up like balls of fire in the sky. Even though it was beautiful, the city scared him because he had never been so far away from home.

"It took time, but the boy made friends, ate new foods, and, eventually, he learned to talk the same way as his new friends. The place that felt so strange when he arrived became a new home."

"Is that the end?"

"Yes."

"Was it you?"

"Yeah, I was the little boy. My grandma sent me to my father when she became too sick to take care of me."

"Where was your mom?"

"She died when I was very young."

"Oh, no!" Rosie popped up. "May I give you a hug?"

"Yes, please." Mac squeezed her and watched as she sat back down. He quickly brushed at his eyes. "It's hard to leave home, Rosie, but it's an adventure with lots of new things to learn and to see. You'll miss Captain Sparkle Pants."

"Rainbow Furry Sparkle Pants."

"Yeah, you'll miss the things you had in Serenity, but your mom is working really hard to make this a home for you, too." Mac leaned forward and said in a soft whisper, "She'd do anything for you."

"I think we should make her pancakes."

Mac pushed himself up off the floor. "I think that's a brilliant plan." As he reached over to turn on the kitchen lights, he watched Rosie stand up, too. "She might need us to take care of her some now, too."

Chapter Twenty-Four

Bailey

Being held by a lover was new to her.

Bailey shifted slightly on the bed, the stretch of morning light casting soft gold flourishes across the linen. There was still an imprint where he'd been—the shallow dip in the mattress, the faintest indent where his arm had been slung around her waist all night long, holding her like something precious. Like she belonged in that space. Like he couldn't bear the thought of her slipping away.

Beyond her mother's lace curtains, birdsong rose, only to be cut short by a distant raised voice.

"Where's Bailey?"

Ethan.

"I told you. She's sleeping," Mac said from the hall, voice calm and immovable.

"Why are you with my daughter?"

"We were making pancakes."

"So, you're the help?" Bailey couldn't see him, but it was

easy to imagine Ethan's familiar sneer curling his lips. It was something he and Hugh had in common.

"I'm a family friend."

"Friend? is that what she's calling this?"

She needed to get in the middle of this quickly. It took her two seconds to crawl out of bed and another two seconds to realize she wasn't wearing enough to greet her ex-husband. She glanced at the wrinkled evening gown balled up in the corner. Taylor would never forgive her.

Instead, she lost critical seconds pulling on a pair of skinny Jeans and a white t-shirt, then pushed her fingers through her hair while running down the hall

There was no time to prepare for a walk of shame in front of her ex, and—what should she call Mac? Things were too far gone for 'friend.' 'Lover' was...not enough.

Racing down the stairs and rounding the corner to the foyer, she cleared her throat. "Ethan, did I make the mistake of making you think you were welcome here?"

"Bailey," he said with a little sneer, and shifted in his sleek tailored suit.

"Rosie," Bailey called, eyes on Ethan, "room. Now."

When the door at the end of the hall clicked shut, Bailey leaned in. "How dare you show up here!" Though she kept her voice low, her hands clenched into fists at her sides, and a fleck of spit landed on his navy suit coat.

He brushed his lapel and stepped back. "Who's he?" Ethan asked, gesturing his chin at Mac.

"None of your business."

"My daughter is under this roof. I'd say it's my business."

"You released your rights to her years ago, and you haven't spent a lick of time thinking about her any of the years since."

"Our daughter deserves more than a—"

Before she could blink, Mac was between her and Ethan. He'd placed a hand on Ethan's chest to check his forward motion. "One step. One hand. Not even one breath had better leave your body before you think twice about how you want to leave this house."

Worried and frustrated by how easily Ethan provoked her even after years apart, Bailey said, "Thank you, Mac, but I think Ethan is about to leave...using two perfectly working feet."

Ethan took a step towards the door and looked around at Mac and Bailey. "I will not tolerate threats. You'll be hearing from my attorney."

Bailey watched as he left and slammed the door behind him. She glanced at Mac. His back was stiff, and he was wringing a kitchen towel in his hands.

"I know that feeling. Like you want to wrap your hands around his neck."

His jaw eased. He nodded once.

"Let's head to the kitchen," she said. "I hear there are pancakes."

There were. Piles and piles of them.

Rosie and Mac must have been making flapjacks for hours. The modern black and chrome stove was off, but a pan with a gooey half-flipped pancake still rested on top.

Three plates held stacks of moist, puffy pancakes, and a dusting of flour covered the counter. The collection of assorted cutting boards, spatulas, and chopped fruits rounded out the brunch menu.

"Wow."

"Right?" said Rosie, "Mac's been teaching me how to make the world's best pancake." She glanced at the kitchen door. "We were going to bring you breakfast in bed…before we heard the doorbell. It was dad."

. She sighed and said, "Let's stick with Ethan, for now." The mess comforted her restless hands, and she wiped the counter and filled the sink with dishes as she talked. Ethan had never been a part of Rosie's life. Aside from occasional photos of their wedding or an article in the news, Rosie knew very little about her dad. That suited Bailey just fine, but now it seemed to make all this harder for her daughter.

Mac went to the corner grocer to purchase a bottle of syrup. She hadn't missed the one already sitting on the counter. It was sweet of him to give her and Rosie time to recover. "What's the trick to making the world's best pancake?"

Rosie smiled and said, "You'll never guess."

"Is it extra vanilla?"

"Nope."

"Is it love?" Bailey drew out the sentence in a long Texas drawl.

Her daughter's laugh was contagious. "No!"

"You're right, I'll never guess!"

"It's the bad pancake!" Rosie pointed to a stack of bronze and black pancakes. Some had sections of uncooked batter, but most had a charcoal crust edge. "See, you get it wrong a few times so that you can make sure the batter and temperature are right."

"Mac taught you that?"

"Yeah. Sometimes things are hard at first, and you ruin them. But once you figure it out, you get the best pancake you never would've had otherwise."

"That's a lot of wisdom for before eight a.m., sweetheart."

Bailey glanced around the kitchen. Her attempt at cleaning had softened the chaos, but the evidence of Rosie and Mac's trial-and-error pursuit of perfection was everywhere.

Whatever he'd been teaching Rosie, Bailey was learning too—one imperfect pancake at a time.

Chapter Twenty-Five

Bailey

"Did you know there's a delightful man selling Gucci purses two blocks away? Out of his trunk," Candice said brightly.

"Hernando?" Bailey set a pot of chili in the center of the table. "I thought he gave that up. Dinner's ready, Rosie."

"There was a red one," Candice added.

"Fake. Or stolen," Bailey said flatly.

"Definitely fake," Candice conceded.

Rosie climbed into her chair, already buzzing. Candice had been in New York less than a day and was enchanted by every-thing—the food, the fashion, the sheer audacity of the city. She and Rosie had already compiled an ambitious list of things to do before Candice flew home.

Bailey let herself enjoy their excitement. It reminded her of growing up here with her mother—before everything became complicated.

"Don't forget," Bailey said, "we've got Rosie's party Satur-day. The venue's handling most of it, but we still need a dress.

And Candy, you'll need baking time."

"Yes!" Rosie grinned. "Can I wear pink?"

"I'm sure Saks can manage that."

Candice leaned forward. "Are you excited, Miss Rosie?"

Rosie hesitated. "I'd like it better if my friends could come."

Bailey softened her voice. "I know, sweetheart, but these people are family friends. They knew your grandparents. This is part of making New York feel like home."

"Yeah, Mac was telling me about some of the fancy people. He said one of them owned a giant farm in Wyoming and had a hundred racehorses! Another one has their own private island! Can you believe that?" Rosie frowned. "Do you think they have kids, Mom?"

"Some of them do." Bailey served herself a second helping of food. "Some of my friends here are all grown up now and have young kids just like you."

"Will Grandpa and Dad be there?"

Bailey could tell that the run-in with Ethan had left Rosie worried, and she hoped Rosie hadn't heard his parting threats. Clinton was ready to bury her ex in paperwork, but the impending legal battle and fallout in the news would be even worse than her current fight for the Ladder H.

"All you need to worry about is dessert," she said gently. "And whether Candy can make enough for fifty people."

Rosie's face brightened. "Do you think they've ever had Ms. Patty's cakes?"

"A Patty Cake?" Candice frowned. "Are you sure? I can't count the number of times I've made my mama's old recipe. Don't you want something new or fancy?"

"No, I don't think so." Rosie took a bite of chili and nod- ded. "I think I want something that feels like home."

Candice looked at Bailey, and Bailey looked right back. The little girl missed Serenity, and there wasn't much she could do about it. Having Candice there helped, and Mac's influence made the change a lot easier, but Sherry's Manhattan town- house was a long way from home.

"It's your party. Cake it is," Candice said firmly.

"Good," Rosie said. "I asked Mac if he likes cake."

"And?" Candice asked.

"He doesn't eat cake," Rosie said, horrified.

Candice gasped. "Tragic."

"He *is* coming to my party, right?" Rosie asked, hope shin- ing.

Bailey hesitated. "I suppose."

"Great! He's never had a cake like Candy's and he can introduce me to the man with the island."

A nine-year-old had successfully cornered her.

"Pajamas, Rosie," Bailey said.

Once Rosie disappeared, Candice raised an eyebrow. "She's right. He'll say yes."

"I know," Bailey said. "That's not the problem."

Candice leaned in. "Then what is?"

Bailey sighed. "He stayed over. The other night."

Candice's grin was immediate. "And?"

"The best," Bailey admitted.

"Well. About time."

"I haven't called him since."

"Not even a text?" Candice whistled. "You are out of practice."

"I texted him the next morning."

"What did you say?"

"Thank you?"

"You didn't!"

Shaking her head, Bailey nodded. "Sherry would have had my hide. She made sure I knew when to show my gratitude."

"Yeah…you need to call him." Candice raised her glass in a toast to her friend. "Immediately."

"Rumor has it, I'd be a fool to miss a Patty Cake," Mac said. "Of course I'll be there."

Candice and Rosie's voices floated in the background.

"I've missed you," Mac added quietly.

Bailey's breath caught. "I can't talk long. We're going dress shopping early tomorrow."

"Oh, really…" Mac's voice hummed across the line. "I liked that little purple dress on you."

She smiled. "You only like clothes with pockets."

"Hey! I appreciate the fine art of textiles and maybe I'd like to write a piece for an upcoming—"

Her laughter interrupted his excuse. "Okay, then, tell me the difference between a hem and a bias seam?"

"You've got me." Mac's laughter tickled her ear. "I want you all wrapped up like a present so I can unwrap you."

Her mouth went dry, and her hand gripped the phone tighter. "That's unfair…Candy is here until Sunday."

"Unfair, huh?"

"I'm going to have to think about that every minute, of every hour, until we can be alone, again."

"Well, that sounds like it's going to be really hard for you."

"You don't sound sorry at all!"

Mac laughed, "I'm not."

Chapter Twenty-Six

Bailey

Bailey hadn't been to the Plaza Hotel since her own introduction to society nearly two decades before. She remembered how her mother squeezed her hand and bent to fluff her skirt before she heard her name called by the master of ceremonies. Even though she'd been stepping into a room filled with familiar faces, anxiety twisted in her gut. Sherry made sure Bailey was keenly aware of the power those people could wield.

Now, she was one of them. Her status and privilege gave her inroads to income and influence that few people could even imagine. She'd run away from it, but here she was presenting her daughter to them like prized cattle. It was the right thing to do. Rosie deserved her inheritance, and Bailey didn't want to stand in the way of it, despite her opinions on the matter. She wouldn't let Sherry's death foist her daughter into the limelight, but she wouldn't keep hiding either.

"Mom!"

Bailey looked down at the bouncing pile of fluff next to her.

Rosie was her entire world. "Yes, dear?"

"It's so pretty!"

The room glowed with alabaster and gold. A small staircase led up to a crystal fountain illuminated by candlelight. Two other longer staircases led up to the East and West wings, where the young women would have been if this were a formal debutante ball. Electric candles flickered and bounced rays of light off the polished stair treads.

Hotel wait staff bustled around the room. They set up linens and cutlery on the round tables. Against the far wall, a long buffet held trays of hors d'oeuvres and petite desserts. Ivory tulle draped across white arches and cascaded down into puffy piles on the ground. Pink roses with baby's breath and gold flecked eucalyptus stood on tall pedestals in each corner, and two florists were arranging matching centerpieces on each of the tables. The soft lighting and gilded decor was warm and welcoming.

"Is that for me?" asked Rosie as she pointed to the large cake in the corner. "It's the largest Patty Cake I've ever seen!"

"It's huge!" Bailey agreed. Rosie's Patty Cake, usually quite simple, towered on three tiers with iced swirls and small iridescent pearl candies. A golden fondant flower rested in a pile of sugared fondant curls. Bailey smiled and looked around to see if she could spot Candice. "Candy did a great job. Didn't she?"

"Yes! I want Mac to come and see it." Rosie pulled on her mom's hand. "Where is he?"

"The guests will be here any minute. Let's get you ready to greet them." Bailed led Rosie past the fountain and up the West stairs to stand behind a long velvet curtain trimmed in gold satin edging. "Taylor would love these curtains," said Bailey as she traced the tassels with her fingers and then watched them shake.

"Mom?"

"Yes, hun?"

"I miss Grandma."

"Oh, baby, I do, too." Bailey bent down to pull Rosie close. The pink tulle on her daughter's birthday dress scratched against her arm, but she pulled her even closer. "I know that Grandma would have done anything in her power to be here right now. She loved you so much."

"I loved her so much, too!"

Bailey held her daughter and thought about how blessed she was to be here. Despite her dad's relentless pursuit of the Ladder H, or Ethan's selfish bid for parenting power, she knew that having a healthy, happy little girl was all that mattered.

"There you are!" Candice popped her head around the curtain. "Are you guys ready? Most of the guests have found their seats, and a dude in a very fancy-looking black suit told me the announcement would be soon."

"Candy! I love your Patty Cake!"

With a wink, Candice pulled one of Rosie's curls and watched it spring back into place. "Good thing, kid. I made it just for you."

"Get ready!" Bailey whispered to Rosie as a faceless voice introduced Rosie to the room.

"Ladies and gentlemen, it is with great pleasure that we gather here tonight to honor a very special young lady on her birthday. Please join me in welcoming, with warm applause,

Rosie Ann Moore, as we celebrate together."

Bailey squeezed her in a hug one more time. "That's you, baby girl, go get 'em!"

Candice reached for Bailey's hand, and they stepped to the side as Rosie walked confidently past them, through the gap in the curtains, and into the grand ballroom. She stepped down each stair slowly, swishing her skirts. As she descended the stairs, the room fell into a hush, followed by a cacophony of clapping. Rosie's smile spread from ear to ear.

"Well, she appears to be enjoying this..." Candice watched the little girl.

Bailey nodded. "More than I did, fortunately. She doesn't know how awful those people can be."

"You can't protect her from everything, but you have a long time until that is something you need to worry about."

"Candy, I wish you were right. I don't have to worry about the people in this room, but her father and grandpa aren't making this easy. I hate that our biggest problem is our family."

"Family is what you make it."

"I'm glad you're a part of mine." Bailey hugged Candace. "Okay, enough hiding. It's time to face the wolves."

Bailey lost count of how many people she greeted with a polite hello. Even though she sent out the invitations, the turnout surprised her. So many people were there to welcome her and her daughter into New York's elite society: distant family members, long-lost friends, and a decent number of interested business parties. Everyone who was anyone in New York was curious to see Ethan and Bailey's progeny.

A hand fell on Bailey's shoulder, and she spun around, surprised.

"She's a natural. Her mama did a great job." Mac smiled.

"Rosie? I don't know about that. I've seen her ride Captain Rainbow Furry Sparkle Pants backwards through the farmyard." Bailey wanted to reach out and pull him closer. His tuxedo stretched across the width of his shoulders and fell into a taper at his hips. He also had a haircut and a fresh shave. "You're channeling your inner fashion model."

"I told you I had an eye for fashion. For example, this dress." Mac reached out, his hand falling short of her hip. "I'd love to see how it looks with the other items in my collection."

"You have a collection?"

"Yes, I keep it on your bedroom floor."

His words trapped the air in Bailey's lungs. She could feel the tight gold fabric of her dress stretch across every inch of her abdomen.

The dress, a masterpiece of haute couture, had an intricately embroidered pattern of blooming flowers and swirling vines across the bodice that caught the light with every movement. A length of silky fabric flowed gracefully from her hips, where a thin, jeweled belt cinched in her waist to emphasize her figure. The skirt was a cascade of golden silk, layered with tulle to create volume and drama without overwhelming her frame.

Bailey's lips were a soft rose tint, chosen carefully to complement the golden shimmer of her couture gown. Under the dim, gilded lights of the ballroom, she radiated warmth and poise...on the outside. Inside, however, her pulse was skittering, her thoughts fraying at the edges of control. And Mac, looking devastating in his sleek black tux with that just-clipped jawline, was not helping.

"So," she said, her voice lower than normal, her throat suddenly tight, "What did you think of your first Patty Cake?"

He stepped closer, heat radiating from his body, and the fuzzy outline of desire began pulsing again low in her belly.

"Trying to change the subject?" he asked, his voice like velvet and whiskey.

Bailey's tongue flicked out, wetting her lower lip as she fought the immediate heat rising in her chest. His voice sank into her skin like a low hum. The ballroom blurred for a moment. Her nerves sparked to life beneath the thin gold silk that clung to her hips. The jeweled belt cinched at her waist suddenly felt too tight, too revealing, but the real pressure was coming from him. His attention, his nearness. And, God help her, the way he looked at her like she was the only woman in the room.

"Why would you think that?" she managed, her voice softer, breathier than she intended. Her fingers smoothed down the curve of her gown, the satin whispering beneath her palm. Her breath hitched because she knew he saw it all...every flicker of desire she tried to keep hidden.

Mac's eyes followed the motion—dark, intense, brimming with hunger. Without another word, he leaned in. His breath coasted along the shell of her ear, warm and electric.

"I can't think of anything else. I'd love to get you out of here."

Her knees trembled.

She flicked her eyes toward Rosie, chatting contentedly with Candice on the far side of the ballroom, but all she could feel was the drag of heat low in her belly. One touch from him and she was ash, ready to burn.

Her fingers found his.

"Come with me." She barely recognized her own voice.

Mac didn't hesitate. His grip tightened around hers with steady reassurance. It was the sort of touch that was both promise and plea.

Bailey pulled him with her, weaving through the crowd with a confidence that was more adrenaline than poise. The hall veered left behind a heavy velvet drape and narrowed toward a corridor lined with gilded wall sconces. Halfway down, she spotted a simple door nestled between two ornate panels. No name. No placard. But likely forgotten. Possibly forbidden.

Even better.

She pushed it open and tugged Mac inside.

It was small. The scent of fabric softener and old cedar filled the air. The door clicked shut, enclosing them in barely three square feet of dusty quiet. Gold hangers clinked gently as the coats shifted and pressed in around them—wool, velvet, silk—luxury creating shadows soft as secrets.

Bailey turned too fast and nearly collided with Mac's chest.

Her breath caught in her throat. Inches. That was all that separated them.

"I—I shouldn't have..." she whispered, breath brushing the hollow of his throat. The sudden closeness of the coatroom reminded her just how crowded the reception hall was on the other side of that thin wooden door. "We shouldn't be doing—"

Mac didn't let her finish.

Two fingers, light and steady, lifted her chin. Her back pressed into the coat-covered wall as her eyes locked with his, the air between them tightening.

"This is your moment, Bailey," he said, voice low and rough and reverent. "You make the rules."

Time caught and stuttered, then she pushed him gently away from her.

Her pulse raced in her throat, every heartbeat echoing the rush that had carried her here. "I just need a moment to breathe," she said, voice roughened by nerves and something wilder.

"Okay," he whispered back.

His hand—warm, patient—skimmed over her shoulder, tracing the embroidery at the edge of her sleeve. The air between them thickened, humming with all the words neither dared to speak.

"You look irresistible tonight," he murmured.

She let out a quiet, shaky laugh. "Says the man making half the guests wonder who I disappeared with."

"You think they haven't noticed yet?" His grin was quick, conspiratorial. "You're the Reynolds girl. They always notice you."

He wasn't wrong.

But when Mac looked at her, it didn't feel like they were being watched. It felt like he was seeing her. Stripped down. Unapologetic. Desired.

Her fists curled into the lapels of his tuxedo, grounding herself in the pressure between them. His scent—woodsy sandalwood and something familiar, like the earth after rain—wrapped around her like a memory. Her blood vibrated with something hot and reckless.

"This," she whispered, "should have waited."

"Everything with you is worth waiting for," he replied, his thumb brushing along her jaw. His voice soothed, but there was an ache under it. A need.

And before she could second-guess herself, before old habits kicked in—

She leaned in.

Forehead to forehead.

Then lips.

The kiss was slow and deliberate, awakening something deep inside her chest. It was unfair how easily he made her forget the world outside—kissing her like he'd waited lifetimes, like the taste of her was something sacred.

She sighed against him, her hands trembling slightly as she clung to his jacket. His arms wrapped around her, holding her close in the dim hush, and she melted into the warmth of him. The rhythm of her heart beat wild against his, steadying only when he drew back just enough to look at her.

"Bailey," he whispered, his forehead resting against hers, "if we don't stop now..."

"I know," she said, her voice soft, uneven. "I just needed to remember what you feel like."

His answering smile was slow and full of something she couldn't name. "Then let's make it count."

For a few more precious seconds, they stayed

there—breathing the same air, her fingers tracing the line of his collar, his thumb brushing her cheek. The world outside could wait. Here, everything made sense.

But then...

A quiet bump. Wood creaked. A swish of a velvet curtain.

Bailey stilled.

Her heart thumped with a new kind of awareness—one that scraped sharp against the warmth and left a chill in its wake. That's when she realized how close they were to being discovered. How this small pocket of stolen joy could be swallowed and twisted into a headline.

Her grip on him loosened.

She straightened.

"We should go."

His brows knitted, confusion under the haze of desire. "You okay?"

"Yes." It was a lie. She was spiraling. Everything burned under her skin—want, fear, memory.

She stepped back. The tension between them sagged like a wire unstrung.

Bailey smoothed the silk at her hips with jerky fingers, the air between them cooling by the second. She couldn't look at him. Couldn't look at what was waiting behind his eyes. There was too much. Too intimate. Too exposed.

What would they have walked into if someone had opened this door?

What would Rosie think?

What would the world say?

"I can't think of anything else but you." Mac took a step

closer and leaned down to whisper in her ear. "I'd love to get you out of here."

"That sounds...fantastic," she said, catching her breath and forcing a smile that barely reached her lips. "But I'm unable to keep you company tonight."

It was too rehearsed. Too careful.

She felt him stiffen.

"I'm sorry," she added, stepping toward the door. "I need to be available to my guests."

Just like that, the warmth shattered between them. Not because of anything he said, but because Mac was more than a kiss. He might be the homecoming she'd been afraid to believe in.

And that terrified her more than any tabloid headline.

She didn't wait for his reply.

Bailey placed her hand on the door and stepped back into the light.

"I know that."

Bailey nodded. "Thank you."

Mac felt the impersonal space between them. "I'm sorry. Did I say something wrong?"

Her eyes darted around the room. Something felt wrong. Nothing had changed, but having him so close to her was triggering her. He felt dangerous. "No, Mac. I'm sorry." Bailey found Rosie at a table with Candice across the room. "I...I can't right now." As she stepped away, he reached out but then dropped his hand to his side.

"That's it then?"

"For now," she whispered, then smiled and reached out to

shake his hand. "Thank you for coming tonight. Please, help yourself to more cake."

Chapter Twenty-Seven

Bailey

"Are you friggin' kidding me?" Bailey almost dropped her coffee. There she was, on the front page of The Globe, with Mac's hand on her hip and a devious grin on his face. She was wearing the gold dress Taylor had made for Rosie's party. Someone had been watching them. She'd felt it in her gut. She'd known he shouldn't have been that close.

In that moment, someone snapped a picture of them. They captured the hunger in his eyes and the ache in hers. Now, there would be no way to deny that there was anything between them. It was on the front page in black and white.

When The Post wrote its article about Mac's overnight visit, she blew it off as gossip mongering. It was an unvalidated source and rife with speculation. The Post was an excellent paper, but she'd been giving her exclusives to The Globe. They were the trusted source for news about the Reynolds family. She hadn't expected an article from them outing her and Mac.

Bailey looked at the clock over the sink. "8 a.m." Maybe it

was too early for a call, but she didn't want to wait for answers.

"Good morning." Mac's voice was icy and clipped.

Bailey woke up feeling bad about the way she'd treated him the night before. Even though the article validated her instincts, she'd been unkind to him. Soft and warm in her bed, she'd even missed having him next to her, but that desire had melted away in the heat of her rage. "Why in the hell are we plastered on the cover of The Globe?"

Mac didn't immediately reply. "You may have noticed the byline. I didn't write that article."

"Oh." Bailey's eyes darted to the paper. Mac was right. It wasn't his name under the title. "I thought you were covering my story."

"I thought so, too." Mac coughed to clear his throat. "Um, the beat isn't mine any longer."

"How? What does that mean?"

"It means that I'm not writing your story."

Bailey sensed an underlying danger in his words. It wouldn't take much to trigger him. "Mac, I'm sorry about last night."

Mac's voice softened as he replied, "You weren't wrong. Your instincts were good."

"It doesn't make it feel any better."

"I'm sorry, too. I should have been lymore...intentional in my actions. Seeing you in that dress...I lost my mind."

Bailey didn't want to laugh. She was still upset, but he was hard to resist. "What about our story? Why didn't we know about this piece?"

"I didn't know they would have someone at the party. A

guest must have taken that picture." Mac paused. She could hear him take a deep breath. "I knew there was a new journalist on the social beat."

"What?" asked Bailey. She could feel the anger coming back. "You knew we had another journalist sniffing around, and you didn't tell me? How did they know about the Plaza? We planned that party in less than a week. All the guests were aware of our decision to exclude the wide press."

"Well, that's the thing." Mac cleared his throat. "I might have told them about Rosie's party."

Bailey's hands were shaking so badly she had to lower her coffee to the countertop. "Why would you do that, Mac?"

"I was pitching James the idea. I didn't know he was pulling me. We needed his support. It was a good story, Bailey."

"So, you did this for the story?"

"Yes...I mean, no. Not just the story." Mac's voice cracked. "For you and for Rosie. I wanted people to know your side! To see what a good kid she is and what a great mom you've become despite Ethan's absence and Hugh's iron fist. Bailey—"

"No."

"Please—"

"Mac, I need some time." Bailey could hear Rosie slam the bathroom door. She'd be racing into the kitchen soon, which means Candice would be right behind her. They had plans to go to the zoo in Central Park before Candice's flight home that evening. "I wanted to believe it was okay to trust you."

"You can. Bailey, it was!"

"We can talk later, Mac."

"Mom!"

"Be right there, hun," Bailey called back to Rosie. "Good-bye."

"Bailey…" whispered Mac, but she'd already hung up.

He hadn't expected her to be happy, and he probably should have given her some warning, but he knew she'd be upset. He was hoping he could fix it, spin it, or make it better before she found out. If he was being honest with himself, he'd admit he was a little angry with her, too.

When he hung up with James, he called his grandma. She'd had a few choice words for him and reminded him that part of coming home meant leaving conflict behind. He thought that was what he'd been trying to do, but handling the story alone had only left Bailey excluded.

His hopes for a family were fading away, just as they'd formed. Maybe he was better off without the job. He could be everything that Bailey needed now. It was something his grandma told him. She'd said that Bailey didn't need a personal journalist. What she needed was a partner and someone to love her. She did a great job taking care of Rosie; now she needed someone to take care of her. He wanted to tell her that it could be him, but he knew she was still, rightly, upset.

In the last few weeks, she'd grown comfortable in the protective news bubble he'd been able to offer her. Now, she could expect journalists to pop up around every corner, and whoever The Globe replaced him with would be there, too. If he couldn't protect her by writing the stories, he'd better make sure the journalist had the right stories.

He'd read the paper that morning, too. It was resting on the dark wood desk in the corner of his room. In fact, he'd read it multiple times, and every time the weight in his stomach grew heavier. James quoted him. There was absolutely no way the journalist would have had half of what was in the article without Mac's loose lips.

James pitched everything Mac shared with him to the new journalist. That guy had done the job that Mac hadn't been willing to do. It wasn't impartial, but it was thorough. Mac knew better than to talk to a journalist without clearly stating their conversation was 'off the record.' James had caught him using the oldest journalist trick in the books. James made Mac comfortable and then he invited him to spill the story. It was going to be hard to convince Bailey that it hadn't been on purpose.

There'd been monkeys, elephants, and even a Komodo dragon, but Bailey was still thinking about the article. She watched the animals trapped in their cages and wondered if they were happy or not. Did they mind people spying on them all day? The animals didn't care about the press. They only cared about their next meal.

Bailey hadn't been to the zoo since she was a little girl. Sherry and Bailey had been talking about a trip with Rosie before the cancer diagnosis. One little lab report stole so much from them. When she saw the giraffes, she made sure Rosie knew they'd been her grandmother's favorite.

Swirling memories and chaotic thoughts made it hard to enjoy her last few hours with Candice, and Rosie was getting tired. Maybe she'd been too optimistic trying to add in a visit to the zoo, too.

"Penny for your thoughts?" Candice leaned over and bumped Bailey with her shoulder while they walked back through the park.

"Thank you." Bailey reached out and gave her friend's hand a quick squeeze.

"For what?" Candice pointed to Rosie, who was picking flowers in the grass. "I'd do anything for that kid. No thanks needed."

"How do you think it went?"

"Aside from the dust-up in the paper this morning, I think it was perfect."

"I wanted to reconnect with our friends here. Rosie needs to feel more at home. Could I be more than Hugh and Sherry's daughter?"

"I think you did those things." Candice waved to Rosie before she said, "You were beautiful in gold. The way the fabric wrapped around your waist perfectly was genius."

"Taylor keeps nailing it. Why do you think she's in Serenity? She could dress any woman in New York. Heck, she could dress any woman in the United States!"

"I don't know. You needed to run away from stuff. Maybe she did, too."

"Yeah…"

"Speaking of running away." Candice stopped walking. "I

might have overheard some of your conversation with Mac this morning."

"I can't believe he didn't tell me his editor fired him."

Can't believe? This is coming from the woman who single-handedly ran the spring cookie fundraiser because you don't actually know how to ask for help from volunteers.

"People are busy!"

"And you're in denial." Candice started walking again as Rosie found some ducks to chase. "That man likes you, and his pride got in the way."

"I have Rosie to think about. I can't take hits because he's proud."

"Do you think he doesn't know that?"

Bailey walked along quietly for a bit. She thought about how he'd run off those journalists, even though they were his peers. He'd shown a lot of selflessness. "I probably owe him an apology, but I'm not ready yet."

"That's okay. Admitting it is the first step."

Chapter Twenty-Eight

Mac

He took another long sip of his beer. Did she really believe he could do that? Bring gossip right to her doorstep? Or, worse, risk her lawsuit or Rosie's safety? He wanted to shake her, but first he wanted to pull her close and beg her to forgive him.

How would he get her to trust him again? Being angry wasn't helping, and he knew that calling her would not work. She'd have to work through her feelings on her own. Frustrated and ready to hop on the first plane out of town, he thought about when she sent him away.

James might not need him on the latest fashions or the Who's Who List, but he'd always have a job telling stories for The Globe. He could go back to doing what he did best...but he knew that wouldn't work. As much as she scared him, going back to the pain and turmoil of war was worse. No. She needed to stop playing games. She needed to trust him. How could he help her do that?

Bailey: *U up?*

A text? Did she think a booty call was going to make this better?

"Pete, I need another!"

"You sure that's a good idea, Mac?"

"Shut up." Mac tapped his empty glass on the counter.

"You meeting up with the guys?" Pete looked around O'Toole's bar.

Mac shook his head before he answered, "No."

"Maybe a half a drink."

"Pete. I live above the bar. I think I can stumble home."

The bartender nodded and pulled out a rag to wipe the counter. "I know you can handle yourself, Mac, but this isn't like you."

"Maybe it is." Mac felt his phone vibrate and looked at the screen again.

Bailey: *I think we should talk.*

"Talk? Now she wants to talk?"

"She?" said Pete, twisting his head to look at Mac from down the bar.

"I said, shut up."

"It wouldn't be that cute blonde you were with on the cover of The Globe this morning, would it? She looked familiar, though I can't imagine why. A girl like that wouldn't be caught dead in a place like this."

Mac glanced at the dance floor and remembered that drunken night. Pete was right. She didn't belong here. Bailey was made for long dusty roads with dirt in her hair. She didn't want couture. Her rebel heart wanted gingham and lace.

His phone vibrated. What was he supposed to say to her

that would stop her from saying goodbye to him again? He could invite her back to the bar, then back to his room. They could end the evening in each other's arms.

"Do you think a fancy girl would want someone like me?"

Pete paused and said, "I thought you didn't want to talk to me."

"She's never seen my place. It's nothing like her house."

"Home is what you make it."

Mac raised his beer to point at the ceiling. "The sounds of your drunken herd lull me to sleep every night. My fridge has three things in it: rotten milk, ketchup, and beer. I haven't lived in one place for longer than a year since I was ten. What would she see in that?"

"Given the way she looked at you in that photo, I'd guess more than you've taken into consideration."

He didn't want to see what her next text said. "Another round," he slurred, as he turned off his phone.

"But—"

"If you won't serve me, then I'll go somewhere that will."

Pete glared at Mac. "One more, and then you're going to bed."

She knew that double texting was bad, and triple texting was even worse, but she couldn't shake the feeling that something was wrong. Clearly, Mac was upset with her. But not answering her texts? Had she gone too far? If he wasn't mad, maybe it was worse. He could be hurt or in some sort of danger. New York wasn't the safest city in the world. Years of being a mom had prepared her for this type of anxiety.

Her bedroom window was open, and she listened to the sounds of the city. When she heard a siren in the distance, she sent up a small prayer for his safety. A dog down the street barked, and there was a baby crying. Rosie had gone to bed a couple of hours before. She'd been missing him, too. Bailey struggled to accept that he had become a part of their life so quickly. At dinner, Rosie asked if he could teach her how to make chocolate chip pancakes that weekend, and Bailey didn't know what to tell her daughter. She couldn't tell that excited little face that they may never see him again.

She crawled out of bed, slid on her slippers, and walked to the bathroom to begin her nighttime routine. Instead, a knock at the door surprised her. "Who would be here at this hour?"

Through the glass of the door, she could make out an indistinct profile. "Who is it?"

"Messenger, ma'am."

It wasn't uncommon for the office to deliver papers to her home, but they'd never delivered this late before. As if Mac's absence wasn't bad enough, she absolutely did not want to be managing a crisis at work.

Bailey pulled her fuzzy pink robe tighter and opened the door. "Yes, how can I help you?"

"Ms. Reynolds?"

"Yes, that's me."

"You've been served," said the young man on her doorstep. He was wearing a backward baseball hat and a polo shirt. He handed her a manila envelope before turning around and walking back down the stairs. Her hand shook as she ran her finger under the envelope's lip and listened to the sound of paper tearing.

She didn't know what the document meant, but she saw the words plaintiff and defendant, read Order to Appear, and her daughter's name. The paperwork fell to the floor, and she leaned against the door jamb, trying to breathe past the knot in her throat. Was Ethan trying to take her daughter?

With slow, steady breaths, she bent to pick up the paperwork and tapped it on the ground to square the corners. It took every ounce of control she had to walk slowly up the stairs, lay the papers carefully on her bed, and grab her cell phone. Her eyes slipped past the Messages icon. There was still no response from Mac.

She wished he were there to pull her close and offer her a hug. She had never felt so terribly alone. Even on that dark night when she took Rosie into her arms and left her husband behind, she'd had her mom's warm home to go to. Now, the home was hers, and her mother was gone.

The phone rang twice before a man answered and said, "Hello?"

"Clinton?"

"Bailey? What's wrong?" He was a smart man. He knew she wouldn't be calling that late without a problem.

"I've just received some paperwork from a messenger. He said I was served."

"Please read me the top of the document."

"Bailey Ann Reynolds is hereby notified by the District Court of blah blah blah to appear in court."

"It looks like Ethan is contesting guardianship of Rosie."

"Can he do that? I thought he signed away all his rights years ago."

"You can do a lot of things if you have enough money. I imagine he's more motivated to be a father now than he was then." Clinton spoke slowly. "I know it's hard, Bailey, but we can handle this...but not at midnight. I'll arrange for my assistant to contact you first thing in the morning. We'll have you come by the office, and we'll discuss a revised plan. We knew that Ethan and Hugh were going to be upset."

"Upset? I thought they would go after the Ladder H, not my daughter!"

"Has anything happened recently that would make you think Ethan has grounds to claim his paternity?"

"No, he came by the house the other day while I had a...fr iend...here with Rosie."

"Bailey, dating isn't a crime. You're an amazing mother. Before you come in, I'll also review the parenting plan we established. It's pretty cut and dry. He pays nothing, and he gets nothing. That being said, a lot is on his side. Both parents have rights to their children, and responsibilities, even if they choose to deny them."

"Thank you. I will wait for a call tomorrow." Bailey thought losing her mom was hard. Moving back to New York, rebuilding her life, and learning to be a CEO weren't easy, either, but those things had been nothing compared to trying to fall asleep while her daughter slept down the hall.

She squinted at the bright screen of her phone in the dark: *I need you,* she wrote, and then hit send.

The moments slipped by with no answer from Mac.

Her phone was ringing. It lured her out of her restless sleep. She glanced at the clock, and it read 7:47 a.m. The morning sun was creeping through the windows, and Rosie would be up soon. Bailey answered the phone. "Hello?"

"Bailey."

"Hugh?" She rubbed her eyes and looked at the number. "I didn't recognize your number."

"Hugh, really? We don't have to sit on formalities. I am your father."

"I wasn't expecting your call. Clinton made it pretty clear that he could answer any questions you had regarding the Ladder H."

"I'm not calling about the company. Though it's always top of my mind."

Her hand twisted in the bedsheets, and she had to take two breaths to relax her jaw. "What can I help you with?"

"I heard the terrible news about Rosie."

"What news?"

"Come, come. Ethan spoke to me and detailed all the reasons he would need to take over the care and guardianship of your daughter. He even seemed excited to get more time as a father." Hugh gave a small laugh. "I didn't find it very rewarding, but it takes all sorts."

"Are you kidding me? That man—"

"What Bailey?" asked Hugh, before his voice got ice cold.

"He's lying about you? He's taking away something you love? He's slandering your name in the courts? I may know a little something about that, too. It feels awful, doesn't it?"

Bailey could hear her teeth grinding in her head. "You can tell that greasy snake that I'll see him in court. He won't have my daughter, and you won't get your hands on my company."

"I can make this easy, Bailey. I can convince him to focus on other...interests. If you release the Ladder H, we can all be happy."

"Hugh Reynolds, you hear me, now. I wouldn't give you so much as a glass of water. I'd die before I willingly gave you anything."

She hung up on him before he responded. There wasn't a darned thing she wanted to hear from him.

Chapter Twenty-Nine

Bailey

She didn't know what to do with herself.

Getting Rosie to school took all the energy she had that morning. The school's brick walls and fireproof doors didn't feel like enough to protect her daughter. Bailey made it clear to the teachers and the principal that Rosie was not to leave the school with anyone other than her and that she'd be there to pick her up later that day.

Did she want to be CEO for a company that was ruining her life? She was eager to hear how Clinton was planning to stop Ethan. Mac hadn't texted or called, and getting another call from her father, or worse, Ethan, was not an option. She'd shut off her phone after Hugh called and had only turned it back on to check for messages that morning. Clinton, reliable as always, had already left a voicemail with instructions to meet him at his office the next day.

She tried to take a jog around the block, hoping to clear her mind, burn off some of her anxiety, and perhaps clear her thoughts, but she couldn't seem to outrun him any more than she could outrun her thoughts.

There he was on the porch when Bailey got back to the house. She watched him as he knocked on the door with a steady beat. An older woman walked by, pulling a cart full of groceries behind her. He shouted, "What are you looking at?" He went back to knocking as soon as the old woman looked away. If she was being honest, when she saw Mac, she'd felt relieved, then worried, then afraid, and then absolutely furious.

"What the hell are you doing?"

He spun around. "Thank God! I've been trying to call you."

"I haven't been answering my phone."

"Clearly, what's going on? Are you okay?"

"What do you care? You didn't answer any of my calls or texts, either."

Mac watched her walk up the stairs towards him. The morning sun lit up her blonde ponytail. She wore yoga pants, but her face looked like she was headed into battle.

"First off, I owe you an apology. I wasn't in a great place yesterday. That's why I came here today. I would like to talk to you."

"I tried to talk to you yesterday. I have nothing to say today."

"Please, I need you to hear me out. I was at O'Toole's late, and—"

"No, you hear me out." Years of holding it together unspooled in one forceful breath, and Bailey's voice cracked with the force of it. "Mac, what you did was selfish. It was careless. You know I don't have the luxury of crumbling. I don't get to disappear into a bottle when the world chews me up—I'm a mom. My daughter only has me, and I only have her. So if you want to be part of our lives, if you want us, that kind of vanishing act can never happen again. Do you hear me? Never."

He flinched, but he didn't look away. "It won't. I swear."

Mac's shoulders slumped, and his head dropped forward. He looked wrecked, and not from her words, but from the truth they held. She could see his jaw clench, the fine tremble in the cords of his neck. Something soft inside her shifted. When he spoke again, his voice was rough and quiet, like gravel rolling down a hill.

"Bailey, I'm so damn sorry. I didn't mean to hurt you. Or Rosie. I never wanted that."

"I know," she whispered, and the confession cracked her open a little—enough for the anger to mix with grief. With relief. With something warmer.

He wiped at his eyes with the side of his hand and then lifted his gaze, raw and unguarded. "I swear on my life, on everything that matters to me now. I will never let you two down again."

Bailey blinked hard, but it didn't stop the rush gathering behind her eyes. "I'm going to hold you to that. Every damn word of it," she said, her voice shaking. "Even though I know you can't keep a promise like that—no one can. However, I still expect you to try. Every day."

"You have my word," he said, voice steady, but underneath, his chest rose and fell, as if her words reached somewhere deeper.

She looked at him fully, taking him in—the lines of exhaustion on his face, how his hands clenched so tightly at his sides, it made her ache. "I'm still deciding if that word belongs to a man I trust."

His features twisted. "Please, Bailey, don't say that. I knew I'd mess this up, but losing your trust...I don't know if I can come back from that."

"A person can only take so much, Mac." Her voice was hoarse. Small.

"I know." He took a breath. "I know things are hard right now."

"Hard?" she echoed, laughing bitterly despite herself. "Hard is an understatement."

He tried to reach for her, and she stepped back, hurt flaring again—fresh. "Mac. You ignored me. I texted. I waited. Hours passed, and you didn't call. I didn't need you to fix anything. I didn't need solutions. I needed a hug."

He closed his eyes. "I'm sorry. Bailey, I...I didn't know how to fix it. I didn't know how to regain your trust. That feeling of failing you—of watching everything slip through my fingers—I panicked."

"Then show up," she said plainly. "Just show up."

"I have been! Bailey, I lost my job over this."

Her heart clenched. "Are you...blaming me for that?"

"No," Mac said quickly. He looked her in the eyes again, and suddenly, everything in him seemed to settle. Like he'd made peace with a fire burning through him. "I'm saying I'd do it again, for you. For Rosie. I put you first, and I'd do it every time." He stepped forward, voice softening. "I haven't cared this deeply about anyone in years. And yeah, I was scared as hell."

Bailey's throat burned. It was too much and not enough. She took a trembling breath. "And just because you're a journalist doesn't mean I expected the worst, Mac. I wanted to believe you were different, and that scared me, too."

He stepped closer. His fingers searched for hers, brushing them with enough pressure to ask before taking. When she didn't pull away, he caught her hand in his, their fingers interlaced like they'd never forgotten how to fit together.

"All I needed from you yesterday," she murmured, looking up at him through lashes still wet with unshed tears, "...was for you to be here. I needed you to hold me in your arms."

Mac's expression broke wide open. "They're here, now," he whispered, his voice as desperate as it was reverent.

Bailey didn't hesitate this time. She stepped into him—into the circle of his arms—and pressed her face into his chest.

His mouth stayed close to her ear. "God, I missed you."

"I missed you, too," she breathed, her hands curling into the fabric of his shirt. "More than I wanted to."

His hold tightened, like if he let go for even a second, the moment would unravel. His cheek rested against her hair as silence wrapped around them, warm and heavy and real.

"This is over," she whispered against his collarbone, but her arms didn't move, only curled tighter around him. Her voice trembled, but there was quiet conviction there, too. "I don't have the strength to fight with the people I love, too."

She felt him tense, his breath catch at the word "love."

"I mean, wow." Mac leaned back just enough to look at her face. His eyes were wide, searching. Gentle. "You dropped the L-word like a grenade and then tried to walk away from it."

Bailey blinked, heat blooming across her cheeks. "What?" Her voice pitched slightly higher. "No. That wasn't—"

"Oh, no, no," he teased, catching her chin lightly between

his fingers. "Too late. Sorry, ma'am. That's legally binding." His thumb brushed the hollow beneath her lip. "You admitted—verbatim—that you love me. This is officially now a very high-stakes cuddle."

A huff of laughter escaped her, even as her throat tightened. Oh, God. She said it. It slipped out, coated in frustration and exhaustion, but devoid of denial. She let her head fall forward against his chest again. "I didn't mean to say it like that," she murmured, her voice muffled against him. "You make me crazy. And then you make me miss you. And then you make me say...things."

Mac's laugh was low, rough, and full of fondness. His hands curled around her waist, thumb rubbing light, steady circles into her lower back. "Babe, you could confess to murder right now, and I'd be impressed that you finally told me what I already knew."

Bailey's stomach did a little somersault. Stupid man. Tender, good, ridiculously handsome man.

"I hate that I want to kiss you right now," she muttered.

"Why?" he asked, dropping his forehead gently to hers. Their noses brushed. "We're past apologies and halfway to duvet shopping. You're stuck with me."

She paused. Let the space between their breaths narrow until there was no oxygen between them—heat, and want, and the absolute certainty that this man completely undid her.

With a sigh coated in reluctant affection, she murmured, "Come inside. I'm not done being mad at the world."

Mac quirked a brow, his lips curving as he pressed a lingering, feather-soft kiss to her temple.

"But you're done being mad at me?" he asked, voice teasing—hopeful.

"I plead the fifth." Bailey smirked, nudging the front door open. "But I might let you hold my hand the whole way to the couch."

"Progress," he murmured, lacing his fingers through hers. "I'll take what I can get from the terrifying, stunning heiress who just told me she loves me mid-emotional spiral."

That earned him a sharp nudge in the ribs and a laugh that left her eyes stinging.

"Come on," she said, her voice softer now. "Let me tell you everything."

Mac and Bailey settled into her study on the small decorative couch. "You really should get something more comfortable."

"Yeah, my mom wasn't huge into recliners."

"Jokes aside, I know that you're worried about more than all of this," Mac waved his hand, gesturing to the piles of paper that seem to have made a permanent home there. "What's going on?"

"Ethan had papers served on me last night. He's fighting for custody of Rosie."

"Can he do that?"

"My attorney says he can, but it's unclear how successful he will be. We are attempting to invalidate his claim."

"I may have something that can help." Mac reached out to put a hand on her knee. "Do you remember that PI I mentioned? His methods are sometimes...questionable, but he's great at what he does."

"You hired a guy?"

"He owed me a favor." Mac said. "I don't know how to tell you this."

"What?"

"You're strong, but you've been through a lot. What he found...it's hard."

"Will it help us?"

"Maybe? It was a long time ago, but it doesn't speak well for Ethan's character."

Bailey ran her fingers through her hair and took a step towards him. "Okay. Give me a hug and tell me."

Mac stepped towards her as she took another step closer to him. He took her hand as she held it out for him, then he pulled her close. "I've missed you." He whispered into her hair.

"I missed you, too."

"Did you say you love me?"

Bailey stepped back and looked up at Mac. "Maybe."

"I'm pretty sure that's what I heard."

"Well, we'll see if I feel differently after you share your news."

"Okay." He squeezed her tightly, then said, "I'm not sure where to start."

"Don't start, just hold me closer." Bailey could feel the tears welling up in her eyes. There was one for every hour she'd spent worrying about him.

"You aren't making this any easier." Mac reached up to place his palm against the side of her face, and his thumb brushed her cheek to wipe away a tear. "Ethan cheated on you the entire time you were married."

Bailed rolled her eyes and said, "Tell me something I didn't know."

"He has another daughter."

"What?" Bailey's body clenched in an involuntary spasm of grief and anger.

He pulled her close, squeezing her as his words washed over her. "She's just a little younger than Rosie. He has been paying for child support for years, but hasn't claimed her publicly. The mother claims she wants nothing to do with Ethan, just his money."

"That no good, lowdown, lying son of a—"

"Your Texas is showing." Bailey pulled back and Mac let her go.

"A sister? Rosie has a sister?" She knew her daughter would love that, but how would this change things? "How can Ethan claim to be a loving father when he hasn't even been a parent to this other child? A kid he conceived in adultery?"

"Tiffany."

"Huh?"

"Tiffany. That's her name."

A decade of worry came rolling back to her. What would this mean? What did it mean? "Thank you, Mac. I'm not sure what to do with this, but I hope Clinton will. I can't change how Ethan hurt us, but I can make sure my daughter is safe now."

"Absolutely." Mac pulled her into a hug. "You aren't alone."

Chapter Thirty

Bailey

It was better than anything she'd ever imagined. Though it was hard for her to admit, on long dark nights as a single mom rocking her little girl in the dark, she would dream about an evening like this. The pieces were simple: her precious little girl, a man who loved every part of her, and the quiet peace of living in a moment together. Often, she'd think about the simple act of laughing together. There was always a bad dad joke (the worst being about dinosaurs), and she'd imagine the joy and love in those moments while sharing her favorite things.

In the spring, it was the smell of magnolia blossoms and fresh rain wafting through an open window. A soft breeze would blow the sweet smells through the house while the cicada sang in the night. They would put Rosie to bed together and then slip away to hold each other in the dark. Those were the dreams she loved holding onto, but she'd never actually believed that they would happen.

Tonight, instead of the warm scents of a Texas night, she

could smell the city. There was a pizzeria down the road, filling the air with salty pepperoni and warm oregano, mixed with street exhaust, and a sweet perfume from her neighbor's dryer vent. There was nothing special about the smells, but they were comforting in their familiarity.

Mac and Rosie were at the old wooden table in the dining room that her mother had lovingly polished once a month. Her little girl was holding a spoon and laughing over an ice cream sundae with a dribble of chocolate working its way down her chin. Mac took a huge bite of dessert, filling his cheeks with whipped cream, before he gave Rosie a pretty convincing impression of a hamster.

Bailey knew it would take more time to really trust him again. They still felt fragile, but she was glad that Mac was back. Thinking all the way back to that first night in the bar, Bailey felt a connection with him. Mac left her feeling warm and exposed. It felt dangerous to feel so vulnerable.

"It's about time for bed, kid."

"Ah, Mom, really?"

"Sadly, yes. Tomorrow is a school day."

"But, Mama...Mac's here." Rosie glanced at him, like he would vanish from the table without a trace.

Bailey felt the same way. She looked at Mac with a question in her eyes...an invitation.

"I'll make you a deal. If you go right to bed for your mom, I'll be here early tomorrow to make pancakes before you go to school."

"You'll come back in the morning? Can they be chocolate chip?"

"Absolutely." Mac crossed his heart and held out his hand.

Rosie laughed and shook it. "It's a deal!" She bounced up from her chair and ran off to get ready for bed.

"Between her father and her grandfather, that girl is a natural negotiator."

"And I am at a bit of a disadvantage."

"Why is that?"

"Because I'm a soft touch for her and her mama." He reached towards her and pulled her close. "I'm not ready to leave yet."

"Then don't," her whisper tickled his ear.

She could hear Mac puttering in the kitchen. The clanking sounds of dishes being washed and cabinets opening and closing reminded her of all the nights she'd spent cleaning up after Rosie had gone to bed. How had she done it all? It was easy to get used to having help, but deep in her gut, it scared her to think about it all going away again.

"Mama, do you think Mac will make pancakes tomorrow?"

Bailey ran a lock of her daughter's hair through her fingers and pulled up the blankets to her chin. "Did he say he would?" Apparently, she wasn't the only one worried he'd fade away into the night.

"Yes," said Rosie, as she glanced at the door.

"What makes you think he wouldn't tell you the truth?"

"Sometimes grown-ups get busy or don't do things."

"Did I not do things?"

Rosie looked at her mama and shook her head. "It's okay. I know you were busy."

"We'll keep paying attention to that and get better, okay?" Rosie kissed her daughter's forehead. "Now for bed."

"Okay."

"Goodnight, baby. If Mac can't make the pancakes, I will. I promise."

"Ok! Goodnight, Mama!"

Bailey walked slowly to the kitchen, using the quiet moment to collect her thoughts. She had two hearts to think about now. Mac could hurt her, she knew that, but she didn't want him to hurt her daughter.

"But what if…it's fantastic?" she whispered in the dark hallway.

She'd spent years worrying, hoping, and pushing through. What if…maybe…this was it? What if he filled the piece that felt missing in their home? Rosie could finally have a father figure in her life who would help her change her tires and remind her that there were good men out there, too. What if Bailey had finally gotten her happily ever after?

She would never know if she didn't give him a chance.

Chapter Thirty-One

Bailey

By the time she dropped Rosie at school, her stomach felt like it had swallowed a rock instead of leftover pancakes.

The slow stop and go cab ride to Clinton's office hadn't helped.

At Clinton's office, the sight of the receptionist's tissue box undid her. She hadn't even sat down before the first tear fell.

"It's okay," the woman said gently. "We're used to big feelings here."

Clinton appeared in the doorway. "Ms. Reynolds."

"You know I prefer Bailey," she said, and tried for a wobbly smile.

"And you know I prefer Mr. Conners," he said, with a wink that couldn't soften what came next. "This is going to be a fight. It may get messy. The law doesn't always feel fair."

"I don't want Rosie near Ethan." Her voice scraped low. "Tell me how to keep that from happening."

"We'll protect her as much as the system allows," he said.

"Right now, what you need is leverage."

She pressed her palms to the table. "Then give him the company. I don't care. Nothing is more important than her."

"It's not that easy. If you release your claim to the company, it goes to Rosie. All that will do is motivate Ethan to push harder."

"Rosie can give it up, too. We could move to Texas, and Ethan and Hugh can fight over what remains of the Ladder H distillery."

"She's not old enough to make those decisions. At best, it would go to a guardian, and Rosie would have to claim the company when she turns 18, and at worst, it turns into a longer legal battle because she is a minor."

"What the heck am I supposed to do, Clinton?"

"We have to ride it out. We need to gather any evidence we have that protects Rosie, and we prepare to go to court."

Bailey took a deep breath and placed both her hands on the table. "Did you know Rosie has a sister?"

Clinton shifted his chair but did not answer.

"For someone who prides themselves on maintaining their cool, that seems to have made you uncomfortable."

Clinton's jaw tightened. "Yes. I knew."

The word landed like a slap. "How long?"

"Long enough," he said softly. "Your mother asked me to keep certain things quiet."

"No, I have trusted you for a long time. How could you keep this from me?"

"I am bound by more than loyalty."

She stood.

"Bailey—" He held up both hands. "Find your mother's key. New York Private Bank & Trust. She kept a box there. If there's anything that tips this in your favor, it's in that vault."

She didn't answer. She was already pulling out her phone and walking towards the door.

Bailey: *I need you.*

Three dots appeared.

Mac: *On my way.*

Where could the key be?

She hadn't seen it since her first night with Max. Paper towers loomed around the den. Unanswered mail littered her mother's old oak secretary desk. A stack of newspapers that contained articles about her or the Ladder H lay on the floor near the window, and a box full of recipes, marketing brochures, and branded swag was resting next to the couch.

One by one, Bailey began sorting papers on the coffee table. "I'm going to need to hire an assistant," she mumbled. When her hand landed on the crisp linen stationery with her mother's last words, she stopped. Her finger traced the inky swirls and softly embossed lines in the paper. "What were you hiding, Mama?"

She could see all the sacrifices her mother made to keep the company running, to care for their employees like family, and to make sure her daughter benefited from that hard work but got to live a life of her own. Was Bailey only paying for her privilege now?

"It's always too much, and never quite enough," she whispered.

"Any luck?" asked Mac as he walked into the room holding two coffee mugs.

"Not yet." Bailey flipped through stacks of papers and started piling them into boxes. "Clinton knew about Tiffany."

"I'm sorry." He didn't flinch, but his face said he understood her hurt. "Can I help look?"

They waded through piles on the den floor. Invitations, contracts, headlines with her face. Bailey slid open drawers, lifted the rug, checked under a stack of old magazines.

There was a rattle at the front door, then it slammed open. "Mom! I'm home!"

Bailey put down the piece of paper she was holding. "Rosie's home from school."

Mac laughed. "You think?"

"Hey, hun, we're in the study."

"Mac!"

"Hey, kid. How was school?"

#

"It was okay. Kash said my shoes were ugly, but Jenna said he was dumb."

Mac side-eyed Bailey. "Not much has changed in elementary school, huh?"

"You should grab a snack. There are still pancakes left over from breakfast."

"Toaster pancakes!" Rosie yelled and ran off to the kitchen.

Bailey moved, started pushing the couch against the wall, and lifted the edge of the carpet further. "I can't let Ethan push his way into her life. I need to find it!"

"Find what, Mama?"

"Oh!" Bailey dropped the rug and looked at Mac with wide eyes.

"What does...Ethan want?"

"It's nothing, baby." Bailey stood up and walked to where Rosie stood in the doorway. "I need to find a key that grandma left."

"Is it heavy?"

"A little. It's super old."

"Is it gold?"

"It's brass. So, it's sort of gold."

"Does it have numbers on it?"

Bailey lifted an eyebrow and asked, "Rosie, do you know where Grandma's key is?"

"Maybe..." She looked at her mom with gentle green eyes and wavy blonde ringlets. "Would I be in trouble?"

"No, hun, but I need that key."

"I'm sorry, Mama, I didn't know."

"Where is it?"

Rosie took her mom's hand and pulled her down the hall. "I made something pretty for you!"

Mac sat on Rosie's twin bed. The pink gingham sheets and lace ruffles lay against his ankles. Bailey crossed her legs and sat on the rag rug in the middle of the floor. She ran her hands through the worn bits of fabric in pink, pale green, light blue, and yellow.

She used to spend hours reading on that rug as a little girl.

Rosie placed a small white shoe box on the ground in front of her mother. "See, I made this for grandma."

Bailey's throat tightened, and she said, "Show me."

As the lid of the box lifted, light glinted off a small mirror, and little beads rattled. The keepsake box was full of items a child would consider treasure: a little bird pin her mother used to wear every day, a slip of fabric from Rosie's debutante dress, a small birthday card Sherry sent when Rosie turned eight, and a collection of a dozen other small things. The key rested in a corner of the box. "Is this it?"

"It is..." Bailey whispered.

"I remembered when Grandma came to the farm in Texas, and she lost her key. I didn't want her to get locked out again, so I put it with her other pretty things."

"That was very sweet of you." Bailey reached in and lifted out the key, careful to avoid disturbing the other items in the box. "Mac, can you hold this and keep it safe?"

He took the key from her and put it into his pocket. "Of course. Why don't I give you and Rosie a few minutes alone?"

Bailey wanted to race to the bank, beg them to show her Sherry's safe deposit box, and demand the truth about her family...but she also wanted to share this moment with Rosie. She wanted the time to talk about each little treasure and why her daughter thought they were special enough to save. "There's never enough time," she mumbled.

"What, Mama?"

"Oh, just something I was thinking." Bailey pointed at a little slip of paper in the box. "What's that?"

"It's from the Winnie the Pooh book grandma gave me." Rosie recited the words by heart: *How lucky I am to have something that makes saying goodbye so hard.*

As Rosie started reading, Bailey smiled...her mother had read her the same line from Winnie the Pooh when she was a child. Even though Sherry was gone, she had not been forgotten.

"Thanks for meeting us late." Bailey pushed a folder across the conference room table. "Once we found the key, we didn't want to wait."

Clinton spread the files across the conference table, the room quiet except for the soft rasp of paper under his hands. Coffee steamed in a white mug near his elbow. Mac sat close enough that Bailey could feel the heat of his arm along hers.

"It was more, and a little less than I expected," she said. "Photographs of a little girl I didn't recognize. Cash withdrawal slips with too many zeros. Margin notes in her handwriting. And this..."

She unfolded the letter and set it between them.

Bailey,

I know you're mad. Loyalty is complicated. I have responsibilities as a wife, a business owner, and a mother. You were so happy at home in Serenity. It seemed almost cruel to shatter that for you. I tried to give you as long as I could.

You won't be the only one angry. Your father must be livid. Don't let him push you around. Hugh has benefited from the power the Ladder H gave him for decades. I can't protect the employees from him anymore. They need you. You'll find all the proof for that here.

As for Ethan, I owe you another apology. I've known about Tiffany since she was born. Scandal, adultery, and gossip...I wanted no more of that. I couldn't imagine how it would help you, but I regret Rosie didn't grow up with her sister. Maybe now that things are changing, Rosie will have that chance. Tiffany really is a lovely little girl.

There are no more secrets,

Mama

Clinton read it once, then again, slower. "Maybe Sherry missed her calling," he said. "She'd have made a good trial lawyer—or a spy."

He tapped a stack of slips. "There's a lot here. I'll bring in an accountant. From what I'm seeing, your father had a gambling problem and used Ladder H resources to feed it. 'Investments' that smell like loan sharks. Unapproved cash bonuses. Timing that lines up with losses."

"He was stealing?" Bailey asked.

"Yes and no," Clinton said. "He papered it as business. But money left the company for his benefit. That's enough."

"How did Ethan miss this?" she asked. "He was in the room."

"I doubt his motives matched your mother's," Clinton said.

Mac slid another folder across the table. "My PI's findings are in there. He tracked Tiffany. If he could, it wasn't as hidden as Sherry hoped."

"There won't be any more secrets," Bailey said. Her voice steadied on the last word.

Mac nudged a single-page document toward Clinton. "I drafted a press release for Ladder H. Bailey can revise. We're proposing transparency, leadership changes, and a commitment to employees. No names or numbers we can't support, but enough to set the tone."

"A press release?" Clinton scanned the page, his finger tracking the lines. "Hmph." He looked up at Bailey. "You're airing out a few things."

"I'm stepping up," she said. "We'll clean house. My father and Ethan won't hide behind what Mom carried for them. Rosie deserves to know her sister without all this in the way. The company deserves the truth and new leadership."

Clinton nodded once. "Then that's the plan. I'll start filings and get Lincoln working. Keep the documents secure. No copies leave this room until I say so. If you want to control the narrative, we'll do it with care—and evidence."

Mac reached for Bailey's hand under the table and laced their fingers. "You'll get to tell your side of the story," he said.

Bailey looked at the letter, the stacks of proof, and the path opening in front of her. "Finally."

Chapter Thirty-Two

Bailey

Her fingers trembled slightly as she wrapped them around the bottle of water, the cool condensation chilling her fingertips enough to ground her. She could feel the camera lenses like heat lamps fixed on her skin, even from behind the safety of the podium. Everything—her family name, her daughter's future, the legacy of the Ladder H—was about to be laid bare in front of strangers. Reporters. She hated that word.

Mac's hand rested firmly on her shoulder, a gentle weight that tethered her in the moment. His thumb traced a lazy arc across the edge of her collarbone. She didn't know whether that was more calming or distracting. Probably both.

"What if this is a terrible mistake?" she whispered, eyes scanning the crowd just beyond the lights.

His voice dipped low in response, more breath than sound, and warm against her cheek. "And what if it's not?"

She glanced up at him, finding reassurance in the way he stood beside her—not towering or guarding, but there, like stone—solid, warm, and real.

Bailey looked down at the bottle in her hand and twisted the cap. Her palms were sweating. She could still feel the burn from where she'd applied heat on her hair that morning—how it curled, then flattened under pressure, how her makeup turned her into something camera-ready, even if she didn't feel it.

"Couldn't we have mailed off a press release and called it good?" she murmured, with a half-smile she didn't feel.

Mac moved a little closer, and she caught a whiff of the scent she now thought of as his—cedar and coffee, with a trace of something smoky. He leaned in, his hand trailing from her shoulder to lightly graze her upper arm. "They need to see your face, hear it from you. It's the only way they'll understand that Hugh is no longer the face of this company."

"Is he here yet?" She forced her voice to stay casual, but she hated that her stomach flipped when saying the words.

"He's in an office down the hall," Mac said, brushing a loose strand of hair behind her ear. His fingers grazed her skin, leaving a warm tingle in their wake. "Did he really need to be here? Couldn't we have left him a voicemail?"

That earned him a breathy laugh and a sidelong glance. "Now who's chickening out?"

She nudged him lightly with her elbow and tilted her head toward the front row. "Tell me—is that the man covering stories for The Globe?"

He followed her gaze, nodded once. "That's him. And I've already spoken to James. We're not giving anyone exclusive rights, not now. But we'll offer a follow-up—with the right guardrails."

"I still don't understand why they care," she said softly, watching a woman in the third row adjust her tape recorder with clinical precision. "It's not like I'm royalty."

"You are to Rosie," Mac said, turning his face just enough so she would meet his eyes. "And to your employees. Your mom knew it. So do they. People want someone they can truly believe in. I've done my best to give them the real you."

"And what's that?" she asked, folding her arms as her nerves pricked defensively at her skin.

He offered her a small, quiet smile. "A woman who loved a daughter enough to walk away from everything, and who came back to save it all. You've got dirt on your boots and grace in your jokes. It's a hell of a story."

Her heart beat faster. Not from fear this time—but from the truth in his words. She looked down to where his hand moved to rest gently against the top of her wrist, thumb brushing over her pulse. She leaned into it, just a little.

"You're sure about this?"

"Remember," Mac murmured, echoing words they'd shared more than once, "A tower, not a gate. Curious asks questions. You let them knock. You let them in. You decide who gets a seat at the table."

Bailey nodded slowly.

"Friends don't spread rumors about you," she whispered.

"That's why we're being careful about who we give our follow-up to."

Bailey picked up the corner of the notecard in front of her and flicked it with her finger. Her voice was quieter now. "Who knew it was so much trouble telling a story?"

"Information," Mac said, leaning down just enough for their shoulders to press together, "is power."

A familiar stride and voice interrupted them.

"Are you ready?" Clinton's face appeared over the edge of the long table, his tone soft but urgent. "Hugh's growing...impatient...and I think it's time to begin."

Bailey exhaled deeply, then reached across her lap and wrapped her fingers around Mac's. She gave a strong squeeze, their fingers locking like seams that had finally been found. Mac answered with a squeeze of his own. Firm. Steady. There.

The door at the back of the room whispered open, the hush preceding the shift of energy as Hugh's presence filled the hallway. Bailey released Mac's hand, reluctantly, and straightened her spine.

Clinton nodded toward his receptionist, who quietly opened the door and stepped aside.

"Mr. Reynolds," she said professionally, "you can sit here."

Bailey watched as her father approached, the sound of his footsteps echoing like stones on old hardwood. Hugh walked past the crowd like he still owned the air in the room.

He didn't even glance at her.

Mac sat firmly between them anyway. Her last line of defense—silent, sure, unmovable.

Bailey smiled, swallowed once, and turned to the front.

Let them watch.

Let them listen.

It was her story now.

Clinton moved the chair closer to the end of the table to give Bailey space from her father.

She nodded and mouthed, "Thank you."

Mac stepped between Hugh and Bailey and picked up the mic. "Hi, everyone. Thank you for joining us today." He casually greeted a few of his peers while Bailey took a deep breath. "We have some exciting news to share with everyone regarding the Ladder H."

"Hello." Bailey's voice cracked as she spoke into the mic Mac handed her. "Hello? I think that's better." She shifted in her seat and smiled at the faces staring at her. "I know many of you have been watching as my family grieves and recovers from the loss of my mother. There's been a lot of uncertainty about what will happen to the Ladder H and how we'll work together as a family.

"We're here today to offer reassurances to both our employees and our business partners. Sherry wanted her family's company to pass on to her daughter, her granddaughter, and any generation to come after that. In her honor, Hugh "Rusty" Reynolds, Sherry's devoted widow and spouse, will relinquish his rights to the Ladder H, effective today."

"I—"

"Hold on for a moment, Dad." Bailey watched as Clinton bent down to whisper in Hugh's ear.

Hugh turned so red that his neck looked purple along his collar. His Adam's apple bobbed up and down as he gulped.

"It's clearly a hard decision for our family. I'd like to offer a round of applause for his loyalty and generosity to the company."

Mac, Clinton, Sara, and Bailey began clapping while the rest of the room followed. Hugh stood up and grasped the back of the chair to steady himself.

Bailey covered the mic and said, "Clinton, can you escort my father out of the building? He looks like he could use some fresh air."

Hugh kept glancing back over his shoulder, glaring at Bailey. She whispered to Mac, "I don't know what Clinton said, but that was the first time I've ever seen someone shut up my father."

"It was impressive." Mac nodded to the room. "We're not done here, though."

"How do we top that?"

With a smile, he said, "Just be you."

Her father's old leather chair felt too large. She'd have to replace the cherry wood desk and black leather guest chairs. If the Ladder H was going to be hers, she wanted to make it feel like home.

A knock at the door surprised her. The phone had been ringing off the hook all day, and she'd sent everyone home to recover from the news announced earlier that morning. "Who is it?"

The door slowly swung open, revealing Ethan standing in the doorway. "Is now a bad time?"

Bailey wanted to say it was always a bad time talking to him, but said, "How did you get in?"

"Joe let me in."

Mumbling a curse under her breath, she glared at him. "I should have talked to security."

"I'm not here to make trouble, Bailey."

"Really?" She reached for her phone and made sure it was face up on the desk in front of her. "What are you here for, then?"

"To talk?"

"You don't think it's a little late for that?"

"Probably." Ethan walked towards her but stopped when she physically recoiled. "May I sit down?"

"I don't think we'll be talking that long."

Ignoring her, he walked to the low-backed leather chairs in front of her desk and lowered himself into one. "Usually, I don't stay where I'm not wanted, but we have a few things to resolve."

"Yeah, like the court case you filed."

"I'll be dropping that when we're done today."

Her shoulders sagged with relief, but her body immediately tightened again. "What do you want, Ethan? I'm not giving you the company."

"I don't want it. The Ladder H is Rosie's legacy, but I wanted to make sure it still existed when she was old enough to inherit it."

"We both want that."

"Good, I'm glad we agreed." Ethan laced his fingers together in his lap. "I'd like to start by saying I owe you an apology."

"A little late."

"But genuine regardless."

"How can you expect me to forgive you when you had another child while we were married?"

"Maybe you can't, but I still need to tell you I'm sorry."

"Rosie deserves to know her sister."

"I know. I've already talked to Tiffany's mother."

"Without talking to me?"

"Bailey, you're running circles around yourself. Do you want Rosie to meet Tiffany, or not?"

"Of course I do!"

"And I knew you would. You and I may not have worked, but we were something once. You were my wife. Even if we don't have that, now."

"Ethan, we have nothing. Rosie is mine. This company is mine."

"They're all yours, but I'd like to help."

"What?"

"I know Hugh was a bad dad and even worse at managing money."

"Did you know about his gambling?"

"Yes, and no. I knew he was doing it, but I didn't know how bad it was."

"So, you let him keep draining the Ladder H for money."

"No, actually. Hugh is an amazing salesman. He really helped grow the company into what it is today, but I was the one who made it great. I closed the deals he lined up; I made sure our operations ran smoothly, and I provided the best-priced, high-quality ingredients for our distilleries. Bailey, your father isn't the man he used to be. I have done a lot of questionable things for this company, but I've never used threats of violence. There is no line that man won't cross. He hurt his family. I don't want my daughter...daughters...hurt."

"Well, I don't either."

"Then we need to work together." Ethan opened his arms

and spread his hands out. "Bailey, I love my job. I will keep doing this, and if it's not at the Ladder H, it will be with a competitor."

"Is that a threat?"

"No, it's logic and reasoning." Ethan leaned forward and put his hands on his knees. "Let me keep building this company for Rosie. I may not be good at cheering during Christmas recitals or healing a scraped knee, but I can do this."

"You know you can learn first aid."

He stared at her. "You know what I mean."

"Maybe." Bailey sighed. "I need to think about it."

"That's all I'm asking." Ethan stood up and walked to the door. "You know where to find me."

"More wine." Bailey said and held out her glass.

"Do you trust him?" Mac asked and picked up the bottle on the table between them.

"Maybe. He's not wrong. He'd be an asset to any other company. I don't want to be a CEO. I just didn't want my daughter to lose her birthright or my mother's last wishes to go unheard."

"Well, it seems there were several other good things that have some out of this."

"Like petty revenge on my father?"

Mac laughed and said, "Yeah, like that."

"There's Tiffany, too."

"What do you mean by that?"

"Until now, she's had the privileges that an heiress has. I'm sure Ethan pulled strings to get her into the right schools and extracurricular activities. Rosie has the limelight, but Tiffany shouldn't suffer because of that. It's not simple. We can't introduce Tiffany at a birthday ball like we did Rosie."

"Well, we could—"

"I'm not there yet." Bailey took another sip from her glass. "I'm still upset."

"Justifiably so…"

"It was a long time ago. I've moved on with Rosie, and, if we're being honest, I won. I got the best parts of her, but it's still a reminder of what I left. Rosie has a sister, and I have another data point that my marriage was flawed."

"That's behind you, now."

"Even if I see Ethan every day? If he's helping run the Ladder H, he's going to be around."

"You're still the boss. He managed Hugh for more than a decade. I imagine the two of you will work it out—to Rosie's benefit."

"Yes…" Bailey's phone dinged, and she picked it up to check the text: *I just received confirmation that Ethan dropped the case. Clinton.*

"He signs his texts." Bailey waved her phone at Mac. "Who does that?"

"Clinton?" Mac smiled. "He's loosening up."

"Ethan kept his word."

"Did you doubt him?"

"No, not really. He's never been a liar…just a sneak." Bailey looked at her phone screen, letting Clinton's text sink in. It was all over…or maybe it was all just beginning.

Chapter Thirty-Three

Bailey

"How has it been barely a month?" Bailey murmured, dragging the butter knife through a softened square of gold and spreading it over the warm slice of sourdough. The bread gave beneath her touch, pillowy and fragrant, the crust cracking softly under the pressure. "Everything feels like it's moving at warp speed."

Mac moved beside her, the rhythmic crunch of knife against cutting board comforting in its predictability. Each slice he added to the salad fell with a soft plop into the wooden bowl of crisp lettuce. His forearms flexed with the motion, and the kitchen lighting caught the curve of his jaw, the short curl of brown hair at his nape. The scent of the carrots blended with the faint cologne lingering on his collar from earlier in the day—something smoky that made her heart stutter.

"The Globe released the exclusive follow-up," Mac replied, glancing up at her through his lashes.

Bailey nodded, brushing a crumb from her apron. "And stock prices are rising after we announced Ethan is staying on as CEO."

"Interim CEO," Mac reminded, the corner of his mouth twitching.

"Yes," she agreed, her tone light. "He's proving himself. But we don't need to put all our secrets on display."

He dropped the handful of carrots into the bowl with a final dramatic toss. "Still no word from your father?"

"No." Bailey leaned slightly against the counter, her shoulder brushing his. "Clinton's expecting something from his attorney, but he said not to worry."

Mac turned, leaning on one hip against the farmhouse counter, wiping his hands on a towel. He was wearing her old apron from the ranch—it was dusted with flour along the bottom, the faded logo from Patty Cakes barely visible.

"He still won't say what he told Hugh at the press meeting," she continued, watching Mac's jaw tighten slightly with interest. "But he promised me—no more harassment. He made it clear that we had everything we needed to destroy him."

Mac's dark eyes met Bailey's. "Hugh cares a lot about what people think."

"Exactly," she said, watching the muscles in his throat shift as he swallowed. "If he exits quietly, with grace and dignity, that reputation he clings to will stay intact."

Mac crossed to her, trailing his hand lightly along her lower back as he passed. The touch was brief, simple, but it sent a bloom of heat curling through her chest. "I still worry he'll take his shady morals and plant them somewhere new."

"Me too," Bailey admitted, voice softer now. She laid the butter knife down and turned toward him slightly, her hand brushing his arm. "But we're holding all the cards now. We keep his secrets...and we keep him in line."

Before Mac could reply, the front door banged open, and the familiar thump of a backpack hit the floor.

"Mom, I'm home!" Rosie yelled.

Bailey smiled and called back, her voice catching slightly from the emotion brewing quietly beneath her ribs. "Thanks, hun. Shoes at the door—and don't forget to drop your things in your room. Mac's here for dinner."

Rosie's delighted squeal echoed down the hall.

Beside her, Mac chuckled—the sound warm and husky. It rolled across her like a wave, settling in her chest. "Not so bad," he said, "being the star of a one-man fan club."

Bailey turned toward him, unable to hold back the smile tugging at her lips. She slid her hands around his waist, leaning in until their bodies met in the most natural, intimate way. His warmth melted into her, and she tipped her head back to look up into his face, her hands flattening against the curve of his back.

"Make that two," she whispered, her voice low and wrapped in something tender. Her words brushed the base of his throat.

He slid his hands up her spine, eyes fixed on her like she was something holy. His forehead dipped to hers for a moment—a private press of skin and breath.

"You're everything I never knew I needed," he murmured, sealing the space between them with a slow, lingering kiss that tasted like comfort, and familiarity, and promise.

Mac set the table. He placed two tall, white, tapered candles in Sherry's Waterford crystal candle holders. The candlelight reflected rainbows onto the ivory tablecloth, bathing the room in warmth.

Bailey made her favorite lasagna casserole, and Mac tossed the salad. Rosie pitched in by making buttered corn and sprinkling garlic salt on the bread.

"I could get used to this," said Mac, as he patted his stomach and leaned back in his chair.

"Me, too," said Rosie. She smiled and gave Mac an exaggerated wink.

"What are you two up to today?"

"Oh...nothing." Rosie drawled with a giggle.

"Can I tell her?"

"No!" Rosie bounced from her seat with a giggle that echoed through the dining nook. "I want to show her!"

Bailey barely had time to blink before her daughter was off like a sparkler, disappearing into the kitchen in a blur of excitement.

Mac leaned back in his chair, giving Bailey a knowing sideways smile and a shrug. "I guess the Queen has spoken."

Bailey laughed softly. "Apparently."

A few seconds later, Rosie returned, balancing something precarious in her small hands like it was made of glass and dreams. Her curls bounced around her cheeks, and pure delight lit up her face.

Bailey's eyes widened. "Is that...?"

Rosie beamed as she set the massive stack of golden pancakes down in front of her. They were loaded—layer after layer—fluffier than any pancake had a right to be, with strawberries tumbling over the sides like a waterfall, dollops of whipped cream piped into tiny snow-peaked mountains, and yes...sprinkles. Rainbow sprinkles glittered like confetti.

"Oh, my goodness..." Bailey whispered. "Is that a pancake cake?"

"It is!" Rosie clapped her hands. "We made it special, for dessert!"

"By command of the Queen," Mac added with mock solemnity, puffing out his chest.

Bailey's eyes twinkled. "That's you, then?"

Rosie gave a theatrical gasp and covered her mouth. She leaned toward Mac and stage-whispered; I'm the Queen.

Bailey chuckled, her heart tugging at the sight of them—that mess of sunshine and mischief she called her daughter, and the warm, grounding presence of the man at her side. She couldn't help the tiny flutter unfurling in her chest.

The tower of pancakes wobbled slightly as Rosie placed it more squarely in front of her. "Careful!" she squeaked.

"I'll mind the strawberries," Mac said, gently sliding a knife across the table toward Bailey, the motion deliberate.

Bailey glanced up at him as his fingers brushed the edge of the plate. "Would you like to cut the cake?"

Her lips parted with surprise, then curved into a grin as she reached for the knife.

Mac's voice dipped low, just for her. "Start with that piece." He nodded toward the one closest to her. His voice curled around her ear like smoke. "It's the best bite."

Bailey's heart fluttered again, her cheeks warm. She looked

down at the stack like it held more secrets than syrup.

From somewhere beside her, Rosie piped up, now practically hopping on her toes. "How is it, Mom? Take a bite!"

Bailey slid her fork down through the pancakes with gentle pressure—the soft layers gave way like warm butter, syrup trailing along the tines. As she brought the first piece to her mouth, something caught the light.

She blinked.

There, glinting beneath the half-cut pancake, was silver—unexpected and out of place. She leaned closer, her fingers lifting the fork, squinting at the sticky shimmer clinging to it.

A ring.

An absolutely stunning silver band, coated in maple syrup, with a halo of petite diamonds framing a perfectly cut emerald center stone, now nestled between a bit of strawberry and whipped cream, like it belonged on a dessert menu instead of her hand.

Her breath hitched as her eyes instantly welled. She turned toward Mac, her throat tight, and her heart dizzy with the moment.

He was already standing beside her, waiting, and smiling.

His smile said everything, all the nerves, the hope, the whispered promises they'd never put into words before.

Tears slid unbidden down her cheeks as he whispered, "Will you marry me?"

"YES!" Rosie shouted, jumping into the air.

Bailey couldn't help the laugh that bubbled up as Mac gently plucked the ring from the fork. His fingers were syrup-sticky, and his laugh was warm and unguarded. "Well," he said, brushing a curl behind her ear, "we didn't think about the mess."

He slid the ring onto her finger with so much care, syrup and all, leaving behind a trail of sweetness she wouldn't trade for anything.

Then, without hesitation, he brought her hand to his lips and kissed it—softly, reverently—pressing his mouth against the sugared skin with a tenderness that cracked something wide open inside her.

Bailey lifted her gaze to his, her voice trembling, her smile impossibly big. "It was...very, very sweet."

Epilogue

Bailey & Mac

Candice slid a sparkling clip into Bailey's curls, the cold metal brushing against her scalp as her friend fluffed and teased another section.

"Do you think Mac will actually enjoy working for The Star?" Candice asked, squinting in concentration.

Bailey gave a soft hum of agreement, her reflection catching the glint of rhinestones resting above her right temple. Her hair shimmered in cascading platinum waves, loosely pinned and effortlessly elegant—somehow, Taylor made it look like the hairstyle dreamed itself into existence.

"My mom used to read The Serenity Star every Sunday morning with a glass of orange juice and one of Ms. Patty's chocolate croissants. She even had them mailed out to her in New York when she moved. So yeah," Bailey said, "writing for The Star feels...right. And despite his beef with the society column, Mac confessed the recipes are what sold him. That and Ed promised he could spruce up the editorial page."

"We'll see if ol' Ed lets him make any changes," Taylor muttered, sewing pin clamped between her teeth as she adjusted the hemline with practiced fingers.

Bailey turned slightly to study the back of her gown in the tall mirror and gently pressed on the row of delicate pearl buttons running along her spine. Soft lace framed her shoulders and dipped into a perfectly sculpted bodice edged in embroidery. "Mac has a way of talking people into things," she added with a grin, catching Candice's eye in the mirror. "He talked me into this...didn't he?"

Candice smirked, eyes warm. "It's sweet of him to move to Serenity, start fresh with you and Rosie. That boy's got big dreams." She reached up to smooth Bailey's bangs, then grinned. "Though, if you ask me, you might miss the big city. Especially that guy down the block who makes the garlic brats."

Bailey wrinkled her nose. "Ugh, no way. That smell haunted me for days."

Laughter bounced around the small room.

"I don't think I'll miss the city," Bailey confessed, voice softer now. "I'm right where I belong."

"Stop moving!" Taylor scolded as Bailey reached behind her to adjust one last button. "If you arrived even two days earlier, I swear this dress would've been perfect with time to spare."

"I know, I'm sorry!" Bailey held up her hands in surrender. "But between wrapping things with Ethan at the Ladder H and packing Rosie's entire life into suitcases—I barely paused this week. Besides," she added, giving Taylor a meaningful glance, "you know I wasn't walking down the aisle in anyone else's dress."

Taylor's expression softened even as she gave an exaggerated sigh. "Of course you weren't."

Candice hovered nearby, gently misting Bailey's hair in bursts. The floral scent of the hairspray mixed with lace, perfume, and the promise of something new.

"How did Ethan take it?" Candice asked, her voice more serious now but not unkind.

Bailey tensed for a moment, then inhaled slowly. "I think he handled it...as best as he could. He still cares more about the company than Rosie."

"How is that even possible?" Candice's tone turned sharp. "He's got a daughter—and now two."

"I don't think he knows how to care about anything other than a business plan," Bailey said gently, the edge of sorrow hidden beneath her practiced calm.

From outside the chapel, Rosie's laughter pealed through the open window, light and giddy. Little girl giggles and rustling tulle drifted in like sunlight.

"I hope she doesn't ruin her dress," Bailey murmured.

Taylor gave the waistline a quick pinch, more reflex than reprimand. "I refused to give her a train. That was my line in the sand."

Bailey smiled but sobered quickly. "She loved meeting Tiffany."

"I still can't believe it," Candice said, perched on the bench, plucking lint from her lap. "What was it like?"

"Weird," Bailey admitted. "They're not twins, but...it was like opening a door to a parallel world. A Rosie with brown curls and glasses."

"They missed a lot of time," Candice murmured.

Bailey nodded. "But they connected so quickly—like they've been waiting to find each other. Pancakes, pets, and promises. Rosie's already planning to invite her to Serenity for a full Captain Rainbow Sparkle Pants experience."

Candice grinned. "And, let me guess, Tiffany's inviting Rosie to go hiking in Seattle?"

"Exactly," Bailey said, pulling up a photo on her phone. In it, Rosie and Tiffany stood side-by-side, arms flung over one another's shoulders, identical grins fused with mischief and joy. "Thick as thieves," she whispered.

Taylor chimed in from near the armoire, arms crossed, her voice soft and sure. "You'll figure out a way, B. Even a thousand miles can't keep those two apart."

Bailey looked at her reflection again, the delicate white satin trimmed with soft ivory lace. It was simple, elegant, and grounded—no sequins or glitter, just hand-embroidered flowers and a love note whispered into every stitch.

"A perfect mix of city sophistication and country chic," she murmured.

Candice stepped forward, her eyes misting slightly, and pulled her into a careful hug. "Just like you," she said.

Bailey hugged her tightly. "Thank you...for always being here."

As the girls wiped at their eyes, Candice began to fuss about Bailey's mascara running, Taylor offered a tissue instead of sympathy, and a gentle knock tapped at the door.

The pastor poked his head in. "Ladies?"

Bailey turned, heart quickening under the lace bodice.

"Ready?"

"He says..." the pastor grinned, "'I have to marry that woman before she changes her mind.'"

Bailey laughed, her voice full of warmth and surety. "He's stuck with me," she said, brushing warm fingers across the swell of her engagement ring.

And she couldn't wait to seal the deal.

Mac took her hand with that familiar spark, that warm, easy tug that never failed to send a flutter through Bailey's chest. "Let's get out of here," he whispered with a crooked grin, tugging her gently toward the golden spill of the setting sun. The evening breeze grazed the back of her neck, slipping beneath the delicate lace of her gown, and Bailey felt light—like a dandelion seed caught in the wind.

She glanced over her shoulder, swept up in the moment, just as Candice tossed a bubble wand into the air with exaggerated flair. Bubbles exploded around them like champagne fizz, iridescent and fleeting. Bailey laughed, tucking her face into Mac's shoulder as a few landed on her nose and burst with soft, cool pops. The scent of soap and summer clung to the air.

"Look, Mama!" Rosie's voice rang with delight behind them, her small arms slicing through the air like she was trying to lasso happiness.

Bailey turned, warmth blooming in her chest as she dropped to one knee—the skirt of her ivory satin gown fanning out behind her. Her dress glowed in the golden light, soft lace trailing over the grass. She opened her arms as Rosie barreled into her.

"It's beautiful, isn't it?" Bailey breathed, pressing a kiss to her daughter's forehead and brushing a curl off her cheek. "Come here, love."

Rosie giggled into her chest.

"Are you ready for your sleepover with Candy?"

"Yes! We're going to watch My Little Pony and make Patty Cakes!" Rosie bounced soberly on the toes of her little white ballet flats. "Candy said I'm big enough to make them like a real baker now!"

Bailey wiped a smudge of pink frosting from her daughter's sleeve with the edge of her thumb.

Mac dropped into a squat beside them, unruly tie hanging loose at his neck, eyes crinkling with real joy. He brushed a hand through Rosie's curls, urging a strand behind her ear. "You'll have to save some for us when we get back."

"I will...*Dad*." Rosie grinned, and the word tumbled out shy, hesitant...hopeful.

It hit Bailey's heart like a note from a melody she'd almost forgotten how to sing.

Mac froze for a second, just a beat, and then his smile stretched wide and slow. He didn't say a word, but leaned in and pressed a kiss to Rosie's temple while holding Bailey's gaze steadily like a promise folding into the air between all three of them.

Bailey's chest ached.

Mac rose and wrapped his arms around her. "It'll get easier," he whispered against her temple, his voice curling into her hair. "It takes time."

Bailey closed her eyes for a moment and held him tighter, her cheek tucked under his jaw, the musk of his skin stirring something quiet and sacred inside her.

"Time's funny," she murmured. "You either have too much of it...or not nearly enough."

They stood there tangled in lace and button-down cotton, wrapped up in the end of something old and the start of something undeniably new.

Their friends lined up one by one to say goodbye, their laughter dancing through the air like bubbles. Taylor air-kissed her on both cheeks and promised to come by to rescue the gown before Bailey could "scandalize it with leftover wedding cake."

Clinton gave them both a surprisingly firm hug, then turned slightly teary when Rosie threw her arms around his waist and declared him "the best pretend grandpa she'd never had."

Candice crouched to grab Rosie's suitcase, then pulled Bailey aside and squeezed her hand. "You look happy," she whispered. "Like, glowy movie-ending happy."

Bailey smirked as she blinked back the sting in her eyes. "I think it's real this time."

"I don't doubt it." Candice winked. "Now go kiss that man and get in that fancy car we all decorated so we get closure, dammit."

Jackson hollered encouragement to a very indignant goat-sitter Mac had bribed to watch Captain Rainbow Furry Sparkle Pants after his ring-bearer duties, before he reached out to shake Mac's hand. "Congratulations. She's one of the best."

He squeezed Mac's hand tighter before giving him a mock stern look. "You break her heart; I break your kneecaps."

"Whatever she wants," muttered Mac under his breath. "Got it."

Bailey laughed, and as she turned toward the chapel—weather-worn and white, settled in its field of wild-flowers—her chest tightened. Her mother and father were married there. She could almost see the ghost of Sherry's lavender-silk train trailing down the old wooden steps, the sounds of joy and dreams clinking in crystal along the breeze.

The blood of strong women ran in her—Sherry's grace, her quiet steel. Bailey wasn't running anymore.

She looked up at the chapel's windows glowing with the muted gold of dusk and thought of how sharply her life had turned—how different this wedding had been. There was no cathedral wall of stone, no crowd of paparazzi hovering for a magazine spread, no father marching her down the aisle with rehearsed charm. But she'd take this fierce, small circle of people who held her close, who knew her mess, her journey, and stayed anyway.

Mac caught her hand and pulled her gently back around. "Overthinking?"

"Instead of writing the articles," Bailey said, her thumb brushing across his knuckles, "how does it feel having them written about you?"

"Weird," he grinned, resting his forehead against hers, dark eyes bright. "I'm still getting used to that part. It's...harder being the headline than writing one."

"Well," she whispered, looping her arms around his neck as

the sun dipped lower, gold tipping everything in honey, "now we get to tell our own story..." There was no hesitation in the kiss.

Mac pulled her in with calm certainty, lips soft, warm, deep. The sort of kiss that lingered, that rooted itself in something unspoken—that crackled down to the bone. She felt his hand skim along her waist, the fabric of her dress rustling like a promise beneath his palm.

Yes, this love was different.

This kiss was steady. Sure. Like a door opening where none existed before.

When they finally pulled back, her voice brushed the space between them, breathless and full of possibilities.

"And it's going to be a damn good one."

About Amber W. Lynne

An award-winning author from the misty, coffee-scented landscapes of the Pacific Northwest, Amber blends slow-burn tension, heart-tugging emotion, and just the right amount of sweet and heat into every story she writes. The relationships are relatable and her heroines are fierce, independent, and (sometimes) a little stubborn, but they always find the right man to love them.

Fueled by caffeine and an unshakable belief in love, Amber has been crafting stories since childhood, drawn to the way romance can heal, challenge, and transform. When she's not writing, she's playing with her five kids (I KNOW!), helping fellow writers embrace their literary dreams, or spending time with her hubby making a love story of her own.

Ways to stay in touch:

- Subscribe to her Newsletter

- Via email: info@AmberWLynne.com

- Follow on Instagram - AmberLynne.Author

- Follow on Facebook - Amber W. Lynne, Author

Also by Amber W. Lynne

<u>Working For Love</u>

Lanyards & Lariats
Toolbelts & Ties
Spreadsheets & Sprinkles
Gowns & Gavels
Bourbons & Bling
Holly & Heartbeats

Leave a review at your favorite retailer, and sign-up for Amber's newsletter, to get more love stories, sneak peeks, a chance at Beta or ARC reads, and exclusive giveaways.

To find more books by Amber W. Lynne, visit:
https://amberlynneauthor.com

Toolbelts & Ties

Working for Love, Book 2

Visit https://AmberLynneAuthor.com and subscribe to our monthly newsletter to receive launch updates, sneak peeks, exclusive giveaways, and early access to beta and ARC reads!

"You've got to be kidding me!" Molly Monroe slammed her hand down on her desk hard enough to make the pens scattered about bounce. "No, I will not wait for him to call me," She snapped into the phone. Her hand slid down her face and she stood up. "He was supposed to be there this morning. To-day. Now." Her Louboutin heels punctuated each word with a sharp click on the polished floor.

Her fingers gripped the phone tighter as she turned toward the large office windows that spanned two sides of her massive corner office. Her scowl reflected in the thick glass. A panoramic view stretched into a stunning display of the Pacific Ocean and

Seattle skyline. Carefully calculated to impress potential clients, the NorthStar Properties' office was perfectly located for viewing Elliot Bay and West Seattle's Alki Beach. Right now, though, the gorgeous view wasn't doing anything to calm her nerves.

Molly took a deep breath and dug deep for the sugar. She hoped the lady on the other end of the line wasn't diabetic. "Ana, right? Thank you so much for your time. I'm just so so grateful for your help!" Half-choking on the overly sweet words, she said, "Please be sure to let Mr. Beaumont know that I really do need to speak with him. Really. It's so important. I need to talk to him as soon as he's free."

The moment she hung up, she let out a long, frustrated groan. The tips of her nails dug into the skin at her temples as she rubbed small circles and pressed on the ache that was forming there. Her therapist had been telling her to lower her stress levels. "This is not helping," she said to herself.

Right on cue, the message light on her phone blinked insistently. She pressed play, not even bothering to sit back down.

"Hey, Molly, it's Paul. I heard work on the Calypso is delayed. We're starting soon, right? I mean, this was already a tight time line for the Christmas launch. And you know how important this project is. The junior partner spot is hinging on this happening. Call me back."

Molly closed her eyes and took two slow breaths. The chair squeaked as she pulled it out and dropped into it, pinching the bridge of her nose with a sigh. Another project delay would mean another headache. And, if Paul thought she was slipping, that junior partnership would go up in flames—like every other promotion that had gone to Mr. Maherson's sons or their

Ivy-league best friends.

"Pull yourself together, Monroe." She uncapped the warehouse-sized bottle of antacids in her desk drawer, popped one in her mouth, and dialed Paul back. As soon as he picked up, she rushed to reassure him. "Hi Paul, no need to worry. Everything is moving along. In fact, I was just on the phone with Mr. Beaumont's office and they say he's making us a top priority." She forced out a light laugh, tapping her desk absently. "In fact, I was coordinating with the launch team and they've assured me we're on schedule."

"I was under the impression that things were stalled." Paul hesitated, then said, "Alright. I need to know if I should be worried."

"Not at all." Molly said and smiled despite her impending ulcer. "This deal is solid. You can trust me."

The moment Paul hung up, Molly slammed the phone down so hard it nearly bounced off the desk.

A knock interrupted her silent scream. She paused, brushed the wrinkles out of her skirt, and took a breath. "Come in," she called, rubbing the tension from her temples. "Conner."

Her assistant peeked his head through the doorway. His curly brunette mop was as wild as ever. "Uh-oh," he said, eyeing her expression. "Do I need to clear the rest of your meetings for an emergency coffee run?"

"*No*, we don't have time for that. I have a few things I need you to handle."

"Okay," Her assistant nodded. "Want me to follow up with Beaumont's team again?"

"Yes. And call back the suppliers." Then, pinching the

bridge of her nose.

Conner whistled. "Anything else?"

With a sigh, she touched the calendar pad and traced the blur of obligations filling her days. Networking lunches, charity dinners, pending project appointments, and a couple of dates with Mitchell. She circled the days, counting out a week on the calendar. "I need you to cover for me, okay?"

"...For the Calypso project?"

"Yes, the contractor hasn't started the demo, yet. We're falling behind schedule."

"Behind? But you told Paul everything was working out."

"I did. I lied." Picking up a pen, she clicked the top a few times and then turned her attention to him. "Didn't your mom teach you not to listen at doors?"

His cheeks turned pink. "I heard you yelling."

"Not yelling. Speaking forcefully."

"Why don't you tell Mr. Maherson what's going on?"

"I will not lose this promotion, Conner. I haven't worked here for almost eight years to let this slip through my fingers. Every promotion has gone to a lackey or a blow hard. I actually have a chance with this one."

"I'm sure he'd understand. He's worked on projects like this before. He could talk to Mr. Beaumont."

Her brows crashed together, and she glared at Conner. "Make sure Paul doesn't find out we're behind schedule." Her hand went to her throat. The pressure of her day was pinching it closed. A small croaking growl made his eyes go wide. "Please. Leave."

Molly slumped into her chair and let her forehead hit

the desk. *A massage. A vacation. A miracle.* After three deep breaths, she pulled out her laptop. There was a new email notification blinked in the corner of her screen.

SUBJECT: You Forgot Me, Didn't You?

Molly shot up so fast her knee slammed into her desk. "Oh, hell."

Seconds later, she was sprinting to the elevator, heels clicking, laptop shoved under one arm. As the doors slid closed behind her, she called out, "Conner! If Beaumont calls—stall him!"

"I was *already* doing that?" Conner called back as the doors slid shut.

Even though it was only three miles from her work, it still took twenty-five minutes to arrive at her favorite restaurant. Mama Malone's had been a lucky find the first year she'd arrived in Seattle. The small hole-in-the-wall Italian place had the best manicotti in town. The sauce was always thick with chunks of tomato and garlic, and , for an authentic Italian joint, they were surprisingly light on the oregano.

She circled twice before she could find a parking spot. "Please, please, please," she said, as she watched as the clock on the dash. By the time she pulled into a parking spot, hopped out of the car, and trekked to the restaurant's entrance, she was a solid forty-five minutes late.

Mahogany wood and old red bricks merged with modern whitewashed walls. Red and white checkered plaid clothes covered the tables and wax dripped Chianti bottles lit up the room with flickering lights.

"Hey, Molly." The host greeted her. "You're late."

"Wow, thanks for the announcement, Fillipe."

He lifted a single dark eyebrow. "Really late."

"Save it." With a quick scan of the room, she lifted a brow. "Usual spot?"

"Yeah."

"Thanks." Walking into the back of the restaurant, she passed a young couple, both with beaming smiles on their faces.

A family with three young children sat at a nearby table. Pasta sauce covered the youngest from head to toe. In the dark shadows, near the back, sat a small round table. Mitchell was sitting there watching her.

"Mitch," she said, as she dropped into the seat across from him. "I'm so sorry."

His tailored shirt pulled tight against his biceps when he leaned forward, grabbed her seat, and pulled it out for her. "Sit."

Words started tumbling from her mouth even before her butt hit the chair. "Honestly, if you only knew. I'm drowning with the Calypso project."

Her words filled the space between them like packing fluff: all the reasons she was late, a few more apologies, and a plea for him to understand tumbled out of her mouth. When she'd stopped talking, he continued to sit silently. Laughter and whispered voices floated between them, softening the silence, but she needed him to speak. "Mitchell?"

He leaned back, arms loosely crossed. His voice was calm. Too calm. "On our *anniversary*, Molly?"

Her stomach twisted. "I got caught up!" Looking at the morsels of food left on the plates in front of her, she asked, "Did you eat without me?"

"I did."

"Oh, okay. I'm glad that you didn't go hungry. It wasn't intentional. Honest."

"I understand. It never is."

Nodding her head like a bobble doll, she said, "We can celebrate our anniversary this weekend." She reached out to take his hand. "You know I love you."

"I love you, too." He leaned forward, forearms braced on the table. "Molly, I've been thinking about this for months."

She swallowed. "Thinking about *what*?"

Mitchell slid his hand into his pocket, and her breath caught. He pulled out something small...box-shaped.

She sucked in a breath. *Oh God. Was this it? Was he finally...*

Then he set it down.

Not a ring.

A key.

Her apartment key.

Her heart stopped.

"I'm done," he said simply.

Her mouth parted, but no words came out.

"Here's your key back. I don't want to do this anymore."

"Wh...What?"

"You heard me. I'm done."

"Just like that?"

"There is no 'just like that,' Molly." He pushed back in his seat so hard the legs squeaked on the floor. "How many times have you forgotten me? How many countless meals have I eaten alone? Our relationship isn't a business transaction." He didn't sound angry, just exhausted. "You keep putting me second. Or third. Or fourth behind your endless *meetings*. And I kept making excuses for you."

"I do! God knows I do, but it'll be a little longer and then I'll make partner. Then this will be something we laugh about. You know, it's just the hard times."

"I don't think it is. With the promotion, you'll be even busier and gone even more. What would you do if we had kids? Hell, did you even notice I got a dog?"

"What? What does a dog have to do with any of this?" She glanced around at the surrounding tables. Tens of faces were staring back at her. Their hands were holding forks and spoons full of food that were sitting in mid-air and the drama fascinated them. Molly looked back at Mitchell. "Please don't do this..."

"It's done. Thanks for dinner," he said, placed his napkin on the table as he stood up. Carefully, he pushed in his chair. "You can keep this place. I know it's your favorite, but Mae's Cafe is mine." He began to walk away and then paused. She reached for him, but he brushed off her arm. "Call me in a week or two. I'll have your stuff packed and waiting for you." Without another word, he walked away, leaving her sitting there with her jaw hanging down and her mouth gaping open.

As the sounds of the restaurant returned to normal, she remained quiet in her seat. The surrounding customers ha d returned to their meals. Then they would return to their homes. What would she return to?

Fillipe asked, "You still want to eat? I could get you something to go."

She jumped a bit in her chair, startled by the words spoken over her shoulder. "The manicotti, a caesar salad, and two orders of the tiramisu. I'll eat it here."

"You sure?" he said, glancing around at the other patrons in the restaurant.

"Yes, I'm not ready to head home, not yet."

Placing his hand on her shoulder, he squeezed gently. "We've got you covered. I'll let Pa know to make it extra tasty tonight."

"Thanks Fillipe, you may be the only decent man left in my life."

He shot her a crooked smile. "Shame I'm already taken."

"Marco wouldn't have it any other way. He's a lucky guy." Though her throat was slowly pinching tighter, she kept the pooling tears at bay. "Can you go get me my dessert?" Candlelight caught the sharp curve of her chin as she tilted her face towards him and asked, "I'll take the manicotti home."

For a moment, he paused next to her, then he shook his head, and said, "Of course," before he walked through the swinging doors that led to the kitchen.

AVAILABLE AT MAJOR BOOK RETAILERS

9 781960 479174